INCIDENT AT ELK RIVER

When Johnny Clinton saves Matt Holbrook from a hanging party he sparks off a series of events which test their friendship, and unearths a plot to seize the Running W and Circle C. The situation is complicated further by the arrival of a family of homesteaders, tired of being moved on by cattlemen and determined this time to stay put at Elk River. Johnny rides a thin line when loyalties are tested as cattlemen and homesteaders unite to combat the threat which stalks the land at Elk River.

INCIDENT AT ELK RIVER

INCIDENT AT ELK RIVER

by

Floyd Rogers

Dales Large Print Books
Long Preston, North Yorkshire,
BD23 4ND, England.

British Library Cataloguing in Publication Data.

Rogers, Floyd
    Incident at Elk River.

    A catalogue record of this book is
    available from the British Library

    ISBN   978-1-84262-637-5 pbk

First published in Great Britain in 1979 by Robert Hale Limited

Copyright © Floyd Rogers 1979

Cover illustration © Gordon Crabb by arrangement with
Alison Eldred

The moral right of the author has been asserted

Published in Large Print 2008 by arrangement with
Mr W. D. Spence

Dales Large Print is an imprint of Library Magna Books Ltd.

Printed and bound in Great Britain by
T.J. (International) Ltd., Cornwall, PL28 8RW

ONE

Johnny Clinton turned his horse sharply back from the top of the rise. He moved a short way down the slope, hoping that the speed of his action had prevented him from being seen by any of the small group of men gathered close to the narrow river.

He swung his broad frame out of the saddle and almost in the same flowing movement extracted his rifle from its leather. Crouching, he ran back up the slope, dropping to his stomach as he neared the top. He crawled the last few feet and peered cautiously over the edge.

He drew his breath sharply as he took in the scene. His steel-blue eyes narrowed and his broad hands gripped his rifle tightly. His immediate impression, when he had first topped the slope, had been right.

A hanging party!

The men were on the edge of violence.

Two cowboys held a struggling young man while another tested a rope which he had just thrown over the branch of a tree. The victim tried harder to escape from the firm grip as his captors forced him towards a horse, held by a fourth man, close to the noose which dangled ominously from the tree.

'I. didn't steal your damned horse!' he yelled. There was fear in his voice making one last desperate declaration of his innocence. 'I ain't been near the Circle C.'

No one answered him.

Johnny guessed these man had already made up their minds and condemned him. He figured that the evidence was among the five horses in the nearest corral beyond the small, wooden house facing the river.

There was stark fear on the convicted man's face and he seemed to draw extra strength from the nearness of death. His struggles prevented the two cowboys from lifting him on to the horse and the man who had been testing the rope came to help.

Johnny relaxed his tight grip on the rifle but kept it firm as he raised it to his right shoulder. He looked along the barrel, taking careful aim slightly to the left of the group. His finger pressured the trigger gently.

The shot crashed across the river. Frightened, the horse shied and the cowboy fought to keep it under control. Startled and surprised by the unexpected intrusion, the young man ceased his struggle and his captors froze into immobility. They stared incredulously in the direction from which the shot had come. Their eyes searched the rim of the rise, seeking the unknown assailant, but Johnny was careful not to reveal himself. He loosed off another shot as an added warning that he was not to be taken lightly.

Puzzled as to who was interfering, the young man's fear was eased a little by the relief. He tried to free himself but hands still gripped him tightly. Annoyed that they had been interrupted in dealing out their justice, the four men sought for some way to rid themselves of the man with the rifle.

'Who the hell are you?' called a burly, powerfully built man.

'Let him go,' shouted Johnny, ignoring the question.

The man hesitated.

Johnny fired again this time spurting the dust close to the men's feet. Startled, they recoiled and in so doing their grip eased. The young man seized his chance, shook himself free and before the four men could do anything he had grabbed a Colt which lay on the ground.

Half crouching, alert, he faced the four men with hatred flashing from his eyes. His gun menaced each one of them. It would have taken little for him to press the trigger. Johnny sensed it even though he was some distance away.

'Ease it,' called Johnny, and added quickly, 'You four get the hell out of here.'

There was only a slight hesitation before

the four cowboys went to their horses, mounted and, still under the threat of the two weapons, crossed the shallow water and rode away.

The young man watched them until they disappeared over the rise on the opposite side of Elk River and then he relaxed. He turned to seek his rescuer. He could not see him for Johnny was still laid flat, watching the riders from his slightly higher position. When he was satisfied that they were not going to return, Johnny stood up and called to his horse.

The animal came to him. Johnny slipped his rifle back into its leather, climbed into the saddle and rode down the slope towards the young man.

As Johnny neared him he saw that he was older than he imagined from the distance. The thin, lean figure had given Johnny the impression that it belonged to a youngster of about eighteen whereas he now reckoned him to be about twenty-four. Johnny was quick to size people up and now he liked what he saw. The open face spoke of a friendliness and honesty. Though the youngster was lean, Johnny reckoned there was strength in the wiry frame. His broad grin and sharp light in his brown eyes revealed his relief at being plucked back from the edge of death.

His gaze beat through space searching Johnny for some familiarity, but there was none. Who was this stranger? Why had he interfered? He saw a man maybe five years or so older than himself, his face browned by the wind and the sun, riding easy in the saddle. The eyes were alert, taking in everything and the young man figured the stranger had already formed some opinion about him before he swung from the saddle.

'Thanks,' grinned the young man. 'I owe you.' He held out his hand. 'Matt Holbrook.'

Johnny took the hand firmly and felt a friendliness in the grip. 'Johnny Clinton. Hanging should be for the law. What was it all about? Heard you mention the Circle C, some big spread around here?'

'Come on into the house and have some coffee,' offered Matt and when Johnny accepted he led the way to the small wooden building where the veranda faced the river. 'Circle C's owned by Buck Masters, other side of the river. Big spread.'

They reached the house and when they went inside Johnny saw that the front was occupied by one big room with two doors leading to rooms at the rear. When they went through one into the kitchen Johnny guessed that the other led to a bedroom. The rooms bore the impressions of a man living on his own, needing a woman's touch to put that extra comfort to them. A coffee pot was on the stove and Matt poured out two cups.

'You steal that horse?' queried Johnny as he took the cup from Matt.

Matt met his gaze look for look. 'No.' His answer was firm and Johnny needed no further explanation to tell him the truth but he got it. 'That horse was planted in my corral. I don't know why or by whom, but I'll guess at both. I reckon the horse was put there by the Circle C either on Buck Masters' authorisation or by someone trying to get in good with Masters.'

'Why should they?' asked Johnny quietly.

'I came here two years ago. Got the land from Wade Gibson of the Running W. Masters was annoyed at the time but he had to accept it. He became reasonably friendly but over these last six months he or his men have become more hostile, wanting me off.'

'You been troubling them?'

'No. I've no need to go on Circle C property, I haven't a lot of land but Wade Gibson lets me run some cattle on his.'

'Sitting between two big spreads and against a water supply could make for an explosive situation,' commented Johnny.

'Suppose it could but I've given no cause to fire it.'

'Somebody thinks you have,' pointed out Johnny.

'Unless it's all a frame-up like the horse

thieving. I'm sure mighty glad you turned up when you did.' His repeated gratitude was in his tone. 'Where you heading?'

'Nowhere in particular, just heading west. I've drifted. Figured it was time I took in this part of the country.'

'My lucky day.'

'Got any help on your spread?' asked Johnny.

'Had two but they quit a couple of weeks back. I've no proof but I reckon they were warned off.'

'Somebody has it in for you,' said Johnny. 'Reckon this here Buck Masters should be looked into.'

'And how can I do that without raising suspicion?' said Matt.

'I didn't say you had to do it,' replied Johnny. 'There are ways.'

'I've not enough proof to put the law on to Masters and to ask the sheriff to investigate on my suppositions will get me nowhere, don't forget, it would be a big, influential cattleman that I'd be accusing. I'd get nowhere without evidence.'

'Then we'll get evidence or flush Masters into the open.'

'You said we.' Matt looked questioningly at Johnny.

'Seems to me you could do with a friend right now. Mind if I pitch in with you?'

Matt stared incredulously at Johnny. 'But I'm a total stranger to you. Why should you stick your neck out for me?'

'I didn't like what I saw today and from what you've told me it could happen again. I figure someone should be around in case. Do you mind if it's me?'

'Mind? I'll say not. I'm in your debt already, don't know what I can say now.'

'Don't say anything, just pour me another cup of coffee.'

Matt grinned and did as he was told.

Matt had just returned the coffee pot to the stove when the sound of a horse approaching the back of the house brought an alertness to the two men. Johnny glanced questioningly at Matt who stepped to the window. Johnny saw him relax.

'It's Kathy Gibson,' Matt said as he turned towards the door. Johnny saw the pleasure in his eyes as Matt opened the door and went outside.

Johnny pushed himself from the table and went to the window. He saw a slim girl whose dark hair, peeping from below a low crowned sombrero, accentuated the roundness of her face. She was pretty and a pleasure came to her eyes when she saw Matt. Johnny admired her sit on the horse and recognised a forward looking young woman by her sensible dress for riding, trousers topped by a neat blouse covered by a leather vest.

Matt kissed her after he had helped her down from the saddle. Johnny turned from the window and went back to his chair.

A moment later the girl came in followed by Matt.

'Kathy, this is Johnny Clinton, Johnny, Kathy Gibson.'

They exchanged greetings and Johnny

took an instant liking to the girl.

'Johnny just saved my life,' said Matt wanting to explain Johnny's presence.

'Your life?' Alarm and concern showed in Kathy's eyes and voice.

Matt told her what had happened.

'I think you'd better come and stay at the Running W, Matt.' Kathy turned to Johnny for support. 'Don't you think so, Johnny?'

'I'll not run away,' Matt put in before Johnny could reply. 'No one's going to drive me out. Besides, your father is far from well, meaning extra work for you.' He glanced at Johnny and added as an explanation, 'As an only child, Kathy will inherit the ranch and so has been helping to run it.' He looked at Kathy. 'I'm grateful, but I'll not add to your work.'

Johnny, sensing Matt's desire not to involve the Running W in his troubles put a word in. 'I'm staying to give Matt a hand.'

Relief at this information was evident in Kathy's face but she put the question, 'What do you propose to do?'

'I've been giving it some thought,' said Johnny. 'No one around here knows me. Those fellas that tried to hang you never saw me. I reckon I'll see if I can get a job at the Circle C and put me in close with what's going on.'

TWO

Considering that the Circle C outfit would be suspicious of any strangers for a while, Johnny decided to lay low before he made any move.

Five days later, a plan formulated, he and Matt lay in cover overlooking the trail from the Circle C to Roundup, the small town six miles away. Matt figured that this was a likely day for some of the Circle C cowboys to go to town in the early evening. He proved to be right and after an hour's wait the two men were alerted by the sound of horses' hooves. The noise pounded nearer and a few minutes later four riders appeared heading in the direction of Roundup.

'Circle C,' whispered Matt.

Johnny nodded and settled down to study the riders so that he would recognise them when he reached town.

'We're in luck,' said Matt, his voice only just audible to Johnny. 'The big man with the check shirt is Red Segal, foreman of the Circle C, Buck Masters' right hand man. If he'll sign you on the old man is almost certain to approve.'

Johnny saw a man whose square, angular jaw seemed to indicate a no-nonsense foreman who ruled with a strong hand, a man who demanded instant duty to his orders and got it. Any Circle C rider would know where he stood with him and would be very wary of crossing him. Johnny judged the three riders who accompanied him were on good terms for there was a good humoured, light-hearted air about the group.

'The others?' queried Johnny quietly.

'Dark one with a scar down his left cheek is Blackie Clark. Tall thin one is Slim Taylor, mean bastard.'

'He was in the hanging party,' commented Johnny. 'The other one?'

'Chuck Martin. Bit of Indian blood in

him. Watch him, he's sly. He's Segal's side-kick and good at covering him in tight situations. You'll never get behind Segal if Chuck's around and he nearly always is.'

They watched the group riding in the direction of Roundup for a few minutes and then Johnny turned to Matt.

'What about the rest of the Circle C outfit?' he asked.

'Tough crowd,' replied Matt. 'Have to be if you're going to ride for Masters, and Segal keeps it that way. But that's the meanest bunch. There's one who doesn't really fit in – Chris Masters, Buck's son.'

Johnny looked surprised. 'How's that?'

'Don't get me wrong. Chris can handle himself but he's not as hard or as ruthless as his father. I'm told there's a lot of his mother in him. Good natured with a gentle streak in him, but he's tough and don't underestimate him.'

'Right,' said Johnny, pushing himself to his feet. 'I've got the picture. Now for town. Don't forget, Matt, if we meet you don't know me. Wait for me to get in touch.'

Matt nodded. 'Thanks for what you're doing. Be careful, don't stick your neck out too far for me.'

Johnny climbed on to his horse and set it down the slope to the trail. Matt watched him for a few moments then turned his horse and headed for his small spread beside Elk River.

Johnny kept to a steady pace towards Roundup but before he got there he made sure that both he and his mount bore signs of travel.

He rode straight to the saloon and found a place for his horse among those tied to the hitching rail. He slapped dust from his shirt and pants as he crossed the sidewalk. Entering the saloon he paused to take in the scene and locate the men he was looking for.

To his left the gaming tables were doing a good trade and the tables in the rest of the room were all occupied. Johnny turned his attention to the counter which ran the full length of the opposite wall. It was lined with men eagerly slaking their thirst after the overpowering heat of the day. His eyes narrowed when he picked out the group he sought.

The four men he had seen riding the trail had their backs towards him and were leaning forward on the counter, cradling their beers in their hands. Johnny strolled casually towards them, positioned himself behind Slim Taylor and Blackie Clark and called for a beer. He failed to catch the attention of one of the barmen, tried again without success so turned his words to the two men leaning on the counter in front of him.

'I reckon a thirsty trail rider would get some service if you'd let him get to the counter.' Neither of them took any notice. 'Let a fella get in,' he demanded roughly but once again he was ignored. The men were not to be drawn this way. He tried to catch a barman's service and this time he was lucky.

A full glass of foaming beer was placed on the counter and Johnny tossed his money to the barman who, in one movement, caught it one handed and stepped to the till. Johnny reached between Slim and Blackie for his glass. As he lifted it he let it slip, making it look like an accident, but being sure the beer spilled over Slim. The tall man straightened and spun round, annoyance at the unexpected wetting darkening the meanness on his face to anger.

'Dumb bastard!' He glared at Johnny.

'If you'd let me get at the bar it wouldn't have happened,' lashed back Johnny.

'You should have gone elsewhere.'

'Ain't for you to tell me where to go.'

Johnny was aware of the tension which had come into the room. The noise along the bar had subsided and eyes had turned in their direction. Blackie moved round slowly and leaned back against the counter. Red Segal took up a similar position and Johnny noted the slight smile which flicked his lips. Here was a man enjoying the situation, pleased to see his sidekicks ready to take it out on a stranger and revelling in the anticipated outcome. Johnny's mind recalled Matt's warning and he was aware of Chuck Martin's slow casual turn which took him round and slightly behind Johnny. It was a movement which if he hadn't been on the lookout for he would never have noticed.

'I'll tell who I like where to go,' rapped Slim. His voice was cold, heightening the antagonism. 'And that includes you. Now wipe me down!' There was a challenge and a threat in the order.

Johnny stiffened. 'Like hell!' He was poised, ready for the explosion. He was aware of Chuck's slight movement taking him even further behind his back. He saw a brief flash in Slim's eyes, an understanding with Chuck.

Johnny's action was so swift that it was talked about for a long time afterwards by those who witnessed it. Suddenly he reached forward, grabbed Slim by the shirt front, and in one fast, flowing action pulled him forward, side-stepping and turning as he did so. He released his grip on Slim's shirt so that the tall man was propelled into Chuck, taking him so unawares that he had no resistance and both men crashed to the floor. As he swung round Johnny's right hand took his Colt from its holster in one clean, fast sweep and Red and Blackie found themselves staring into the cold muzzle of a Colt.

'What sort of a hick town is this where you can't get a quiet drink without trouble?' he snarled, his eyes smoking with fury and boiling ill for anyone who tried him further. The two men sprawling on the floor eyed him with an anger deepened by an injured pride. He read their minds. 'I wouldn't try anything, you'll get your brains blown out.'

Johnny saw some of the tension evaporate from Red Segal. A slightly amused expression had come to his eyes and Johnny knew he was highly entertained by seeing his men outsmarted. Johnny glanced at him. The situation was just as he wanted it. 'What sort of sidekicks do you ride with? Can't stand up for themselves. Tall fella frightened to take me on unless he had that other bastard behind me. You scared of taking anyone on yourself?' The words were challenging, taunting and Johnny was aware of the tense silence which had come over the saloon. He realised that everyone was poised, eager to see the outcome of a challenge which had never been directed at Red Segal before.

Red also knew it. There was a tricky situation to handle. He must not be seen to back down if he wanted to keep his position of tough authority in Roundup.

He looked at Johnny with cold, calculating eyes. A cool brain was sizing up the man who held the upper hand and weighing up the possibility of coming out of this situation with his reputation intact.

Suddenly the coldness disappeared and in its place Johnny saw the amusement return. Red's lips split into a broad smile and he started to laugh loudly. For one brief moment the tension in the saloon heightened and then suddenly subsided, drawn away by Red's loud laughter. But Johnny kept alert, not wanting any of these men to have the slightest chance of coming back at him, and he knew that Red was aware of his continued precaution. 'Put your gun up and come and have a drink on me.' Red continued to chuckle.

'Not till I see you really do have these numbskulls at a word.'

'All right,' said Red. 'Back off him, boys.'

Morose, and sullen, Slim and Chuck scrambled to their feet and reluctantly joined Blackie who had turned back to the bar. 'You sure know how to handle yourself, want a job?'

The incident was over. Cowboys returned to the drinks and gambling, while others redirected their interrupted attention to the saloon girls. Johnny slipped his gun back into its holster.

'Only job I want right now is to teach some fella back at the river a lesson.' Johnny had forced Slim to edge along the bar to make room for him next to Red. He accepted the beer which Red had ordered for him.

'Who's that?' queried Red, falling for the

bait which Johnny had dangled.

'Don't know. I was riding along peaceable, cutting across the higher part of the river not far from a small wooden house, when this coyote took a shot at me. He warned me to keep away from his spread. Told him I was just heading for town, but didn't seem to make any difference to his hornery nature. So I kept on riding, didn't want to get too near that rifle 'cos that fella was sure jumpy.'

'That's Matt Holbrook,' said Red. 'If you want to get evens with him you ride for me. You'll be doing us both a favour. I can use a man who can handle himself.'

'And who are you?' queried Johnny.

'Red Segal, foreman of the Circle C.'

'Maybe your boss won't take me on.'

'He will. We agree on most things.'

'Don't want a job permanent but I'll have it for a few months.'

'Right. You're on,' said Red.

Johnny introduced himself and when Red named his sidekicks they nodded sullenly at the man who had humiliated them, but

31

knew they dare not buck against him when their boss had taken a liking to him.

Although he was tuned to this situation, Johnny knew he would have to stay alert, especially to any action by Slim and Chuck for he figured they would not forget the incident in the saloon.

THREE

When he reached the Circle C with Red Segal, Johnny was taken straight to the ranch-house and introduced to Buck Masters, and Johnny noted that Red did not give his boss any details of what had happened in the saloon. Buck eyed him up and down and the broad, thick-set owner of the Circle C approved Red's action.

Red pointed out the bunk-house and then told Johnny that he'd a special job for him in the morning. 'I want you around the ranch-house. I'll be taking the men to do some rounding up prior to branding, boss ain't coming. I want you to keep an eye on him.'

'What for?' Johnny queried, surprised at his assignment.

'That fella that took a shot at you, well we had some trouble with him the other day.

33

Boss doesn't know about it, but Holbrook doesn't know that and he just might figure the boss did and come gunning for him.'

'So you want me to tail the boss all day and watch out for Holbrook.'

'That's about the size of it. But don't let the boss know you're protecting him, he'd go sky high and want to know why he was being nursemaided.'

'This something personal between you and Holbrook?' queried Johnny hoping to get a lead on the vendetta against Matt.

'No. You've seen where he is, well boss doesn't like it, our water supply could be threatened any time.'

'How come Holbrook's there in the first place?'

'He isn't on Circle C land. The other side of the river belongs to Running W and old man Gibson let Holbrook have some land. Buck objected at the time but there was nothing he could do.'

'So you're doing it to keep in with the boss?'

'Well...' Red left the question unanswered and walked away.

Johnny found his bunk and met the rest of the Circle C riders and figured Matt's summing up of them was accurate. He lay awake for a while turning over Red's conversation, and he figured that while Buck Masters wanted Matt out of the way, because of the threat to water supplies, he was not one to go as far as a hanging party, that had been Red's doing, interpreting Buck's desire to its ultimate. Johnny knew that so long as Red was around Matt's life was in danger. His task of finding out why Matt was threatened had been easier than he expected.

But he wondered, had it been too easy? Why had Red been so open to him, a stranger? Was there more behind the threats to Matt than Red had led him to believe? And had he really fooled the foreman?

Johnny decided that, although he knew Matt was not gunning for Buck Masters, he had to make a pretence of carrying out Red's orders. The foreman could easily order one of his sidekicks to double back and check on him.

After watching the Circle C riders, led by Red Segal, leave, Johnny started to check the lay-out of the Circle C buildings. The bunk-house was situated to the left of the ranch-house and the stable stood on a slight elevation of the ground a short distance behind the bunk-house. When Johnny climbed into the loft at one end of the stable he realised that the rise in the ground coupled with his height in the stable gave him a good view of the ranch-house and the surrounding area. If Red Segal checked on him it would appear that he was in a perfect position to watch Masters, the house was in full view and if Masters left the ranch he would have to come to the stable for a horse. To be ready for such an occurrence Johnny decided to have his own horse ready.

About a mile from the ranch Red Segal pulled Slim Taylor and Chuck Martin out of the bunch of riders and told the rest to ride on.

'You two still seething because I signed Clinton on instead of backing you to the point of a gun-fight.' Red's words were more of a statement than a question. 'Ain't the best place to have someone you want to teach a lesson right with you?'

'I didn't see Clinton in that bunch of riders,' remarked Slim sarcastically.

Red stiffened, his eyes narrowed. 'Do you take me for a clown?' he rapped harshly.

'No, boss, no.' Slim hastened to reassure him, knowing that he had come close to annoying Red with his comment.

'Well, the pair of you listen carefully. I've set Clinton up for you. I left him back at the ranch to keep an eye on Masters. I made out I thought Holbrook might come gunning for him.' He noted the look of satisfaction cross their faces and their eyes light up with the thought of revenge. 'I figure there's more to Clinton than there appears. He could have gone anywhere at that bar but he chose us and that spilling of the beer, I happened to be watching him take hold of that beer, it

was no accident, Clinton spilled it on pur-
pose.'

'What for?' asked Chuck.

'I figure he wanted to pick a quarrel to try
to do what he did, get in with us.'

'If that's so then he was taking a risk.'

'No, just mighty confident in his own
ability. And you two found he was right.'

'Why should he want to get in with us?'
queried Slim.

'You remember he said Holbrook had
taken a shot at him? Well that could be a
bluff. We've never had any trace of that
hombre that broke up the hanging party, it
could be Clinton. So I figured just in case
I'm right, to take the precaution of eliminat-
ing him.'

Slim grinned. 'Leave it to us.'

'It'll be a pleasure,' said Chuck already
savouring the forthcoming confrontation
with Johnny.

'Make sure you get it right this time.' Red
eyed the two men, turned his horse and
galloped after the Circle C riders.

Slim and Chuck grinned at each other and sent their mounts in the direction of the ranch.

About a quarter of a mile from the ranch, before they came in sight of the buildings, they left their horses and ran to the top of the rise from which they watched for some sign of Johnny. After only a few minutes Slim nudged Chuck and pointed to the bunk-house. Their luck was in! Johnny had appeared and was now walking towards the stables carrying his saddle-bags.

'Got him!' grinned Slim when Johnny went inside.

'Sure have,' returned Chuck.

The two men, needing to reach the stable without being detected, hurried in a half run towards the building.

Inside, Johnny saddled his horse and, when everything was to his satisfaction, he returned to the loft to resume his watch, un-aware that two men were running towards the back of the stable.

Johnny had just settled himself when the back door of the ranch-house opened and a young man hurried out. He was tall and well-built with it. Annoyance clouded a face which otherwise would have been open and pleasant. Johnny figured he was looking at Buck Masters' son, Chris, a point which was verified when Buck appeared at the door and Chris threw over his shoulder, 'Dad, we've had this out before. There's nothing more to say.'

'I think there's a hell of a lot to say.' Buck's voice boomed angrily as he hurried after his son.

They came into the stable and Chris went to a horse which he started to saddle. His father moved in his way.

'Don't be a fool, Chris. What sort of a man are you to let some little upstart like Holbrook step in? Haven't you got any pride?'

'Pride has nothing to do with it,' Chris retorted. 'You're forgetting that there's another person involved, Kathy.'

'If I know Kathy she'd rather have you

than Holbrook if you'd assert yourself.'

'I figure I know her better than you,' stormed Chris. 'And I respect her feelings. Trouble with you is that because Kathy and I have been together all our lives you thought marriage between us would follow. Well you're wrong, Kathy's found someone else.'

'I said he'd be trouble when old Wade Gibson let him have some of Running W land but I never thought it would be trouble of this sort. Good grief, you could have had Kathy. Don't know what you've been thinking about, good looking girl like that and the heir to the Running W, you'd have had the biggest spread in Montana with Circle C and Running W joined together. You're a fool, Chris.'

'That's the real reason you're angry over this isn't it? Kathy's father's ailing and you figure that before long you'd be running the two ranches if I was married to Kathy.' Chris saw the false protests springing to his father's lips. 'Don't tell me otherwise. Oh, we'd get along alright, we've known each other all our lives. But I respect her feelings and won't interfere in this.'

'There are ways,' rapped Buck and with one final glare at his son swung on his heels and hurried from the stable. Chris, regretting their differences, watched his father for a moment then continued saddling his horse.

Slim and Chuck were close to the single door at the back of the stable when they heard voices raised in anger. Recognising them as Buck and Chris, they flattened themselves on either side of the door and listened. The voices ceased and Slim and Chuck exchanged glances. From what they had heard they relished the thought of revealing the information to Red, but first they had to deal with Clinton. Slim peered through a crack in the woodwork and saw Chris saddling his horse.

A few moments later Chris rode from the stable and headed for Roundup.

Johnny remained in the loft. It suited him

to carry out Red's orders to watch Masters, but his thoughts were on what he had just heard. So the supposed threat by Matt to the water supply was only part of the story. Buck had hoped for bigger things and the fact that Kathy had fallen for Matt had upset his ambitions. Johnny wondered just how much of this Red Segal knew.

Johnny's thoughts were suddenly interrupted. Johnny tensed. Had he been mistaken or had he heard a slight squeak? He listened intently but the sound did not come again. Still alert he took in the building quickly searching for something which might give him a clue to the sound. His eyes moved along the back of the stable and were arrested by the sight of a small area where the gloom had been lightened. He watched it and saw it darken again. Someone had opened and closed a door, the single door he recalled seeing at the rear of the building.

Someone didn't want his presence known. Someone gunning for him? Slim, Chuck sneaked away from the others and come back to take revenge for their humiliation in the saloon? Johnny was alert to all possibilities. Had they returned on Red's prompting, perhaps Red hadn't been fooled and had lulled him in to joining the Circle C so that he could set him up for just a situation like this. Now he reflected, it had all been too easy.

Johnny moved quickly but silently across the small floor of the loft to the loading opening. He glanced across at the house. There was no sign of Buck, and Johnny hoped that the ranch owner had no cause to come to the back of the house for the next few minutes.

Johnny sat down on the floor, turned and lowered himself out of the building until he was hanging by the full length of his arms. He relaxed then suddenly released his grip. He plummeted to the ground, allowing himself to roll as soon as his feet touched the ground. He tumbled over and almost in the same movement came to his feet, thankful he had been spared a broken ankle or twisted knee.

He hesitated fractionally, listening. No sound came from the stable. He cast a quick glance in the direction of the house. All was still. He moved quickly to the open doors, dropped to his stomach and using the cover of the side of the first stall moved swiftly out of the bright light into the gloom of the stable.

The building had stalls along two walls with two more sets backing on to each other down the centre. Two, wide, open ways separated the outer stalls from those on the inside. Johnny peered cautiously round the woodwork along the open way but there was no sign of anyone. He guessed they must be using the other.

Johnny moved swiftly to the first inside stall and listened, his ears tuned for the slightest sound. All was quiet. With gun drawn he waited. He needed to have some location on his adversaries before he acted. He wanted them to reveal their presence rather than he give his away.

Once inside the stable, Slim and Chuck took cover behind the nearest stall and let their eyes become accustomed to the change of light. Once they had done that they moved into the open way and proceeded slowly and carefully examining each stall in turn while the other one covered him. Nearing the end of the stalls Slim indicated that he would go round to the right to the other row of stalls while Chuck covered the loft. Slim did not want his back exposed as he moved away from the loft. Chuck nodded his understanding and Slim moved towards the next row of stalls.

They had been so quiet about their progress that Johnny, crouching behind the woodwork of the stall was only aware of Slim's nearness when he heard his breathing on the other side of the wood. Johnny tensed himself. Any moment Slim would come round the corner.

Johnny's action was swift, hard and sure. Even as Slim's eyes widened with the surprise of discovery, and his lips moved to shout, Johnny struck. The Colt came hard on to Slim's forehead and he pitched to the floor without a murmur. Johnny knew the thump as the unconscious man hit the floor would alert Chuck. He had to act quickly so that Chuck would not have time to think, so that nothing would arouse his suspicions.

'Got him!' called Johnny quietly, hoping that Chuck would act without thinking.

Chuck did just as Johnny expected. He hurried to join Slim. He came round the corner quickly, pulling up sharply when he saw the huddled form on the floor. In the split second that it took to register on Chuck's mind that this was Slim lying on the floor Johnny was already striking. Chuck looked up in amazed surprise only to see in one brief moment the barrel of a Colt coming up in a fast sweep. It took him full on the chin, propelling him backwards and driving him into unconsciousness before he hit the floor.

One quick look told Johnny that the two

men would be out of this world for some time. He figured that things would be too hot for him around the Circle C now, he had to play things as if Red suspected him and had sent Slim and Chuck to deal with him.

He hurried to the bunk-house, collected his belongings and in a few minutes was riding away from the Circle C in the direction of Elk River.

When he topped the rise overlooking Matt's holding he pulled sharply to a halt, surprised by the sight of three wagons at the top of the slope behind the house.

He took in the scene swiftly and saw several people outside Matt's house in what appeared to be friendly conversation. He put his horse down the slope to the river and his movement attracted the attention of the people of the opposite side of the river.

'Johnny Clinton, friend of mine,' Matt reassured his visitors when he saw Johnny clear the water and make towards them. An anxiety and curiosity gripped Matt. Johnny was back soon and with saddle-bags and blankets, it looked as if he was going to stay.

Matt and Johnny greeted each other as Johnny pulled his horse to a stop in front of the small house. Johnny could tell that Matt was anxious to hear his news but that would have to wait with strangers about.

'Johnny meet Bill Webster.' Johnny found his hand taken in the firm grip of a well-built man whose body had been strengthened by a life of hard, out-of-doors work. His face was friendly and open and there was a smile on his lips. 'His wife, Lydia. His daughter, Rhona and two sons Ed and Kemp.'

Johnny exchanged greetings with them all and liked what he saw. He detected even in this brief meeting that they were a close family and everyone would back the other up no matter what.

'Homesteaders!' said Matt.

'That's all we need,' remarked Johnny.

FOUR

'What do you mean?' There was a touch-iness in Bill Webster's voice and a little of the friendliness had gone from his eyes as he faced Johnny.

He glanced round the newcomers and saw a worried concern in the two women and a tension in Webster's two sons. 'Just that we've enough trouble around here at the moment without adding homesteaders to it.'

'I'm only small,' Matt put in quickly as an explanation. 'I've been having trouble with the big spread on the other side of the river, the Circle C. I don't think they'd be any too friendly towards homesteaders.'

'We're getting tired of moving on,' said Bill. 'We figured we'd settle in the next place for good and if we found cattlemen hostile we'd try to stick it out. We heard that we might get sympathy from Wade Gibson. Thought it might be you when we saw your house.'

'Wade Gibson runs the Running W, he could be sympathetic, he was towards me.'

'From what Matt has told me I believe Wade would help you, but I figure I must warn you that even though Gibson might be sympathetic I doubt if Buck Masters or any of the Circle C riders will be friendly towards you.'

'But if we were on Gibson's land...'

'Wouldn't make any difference,' cut in Johnny. 'He'd see you as a threat to cattlemen and do all in his power to move you on.'

'We've met the like of him before and always moved on. This time with a sympathetic cattleman and yourselves I figure it's worth trying to resist Masters' efforts to get rid of us.' Bill glanced round his family and knew from their looks that he had their approval and backing. 'Now if you'll direct me to Wade Gibson's place I'll see if I can strike up a friendly note with him.'

Matt started to issue directions when he was interrupted by Johnny. 'There may be no need for you to go.' He indicated a rider coming down the slope to the house.

'A girl.' Webster's remark contained an unspoken query of how can she help?

'Kathy Gibson,' explained Matt. 'Wade's daughter. Wade is not well, hasn't been for some time so Kathy, along with their foreman, Frank Sommers, runs the Running W.'

Matt made the introductions and, once they were over, Bill Webster put his case to Kathy.

'Well,' said Kathy when Bill had finished, 'some of the cattlemen around here aren't going to be too happy about settling homesteaders, in fact some of them will be downright antagonistic but if you want to risk that then I figure we can fix you up.'

The exchange of smiles around the family spoke of their delight. Here were some friendly cattle people and now they had a chance of making a permanent home. They were determined to seize it with both hands.

'We're mighty grateful to you, miss,' said Bill, his face broken by a broad smile.

'If we're going to be neighbours and friendly, then it's Kathy, please. Now how about all of you coming over to the Running W this evening for a meal. Meet my pa and get to know each other a little better. That goes for you Matt and Johnny.'

'That's mighty nice of you, Kathy,' smiled Bill. 'We'll be delighted to come.'

'Good, now I'd better show you where you can settle. You like to come along, Matt?'

'Sure,' agreed Matt.

When Johnny was asked the same question he refused saying he would like to get settled in.

As the party was preparing to leave Matt seized a brief opportunity to have a word with Johnny. 'What happened? Why are you back?'

'Smart guy that Segal. He tumbled to me, at least I figure he did. Tell you about it when you get back.'

Matt had to be contented with that brief explanation as the Websters were ready to leave. Johnny watched them go with mixed feelings about the coming of the home-steaders and wondering about the complications it might add to the present situation.

Slim stirred at the pounding in his mind. His hazy senses tried to concentrate on what it was all about. His eyes flickered then closed again. The light hurt. He moved his arm, wanting to feel his throbbing temple, wanting to bring it some ease. What had happened? His brain tried to force a question and answer it. He opened his eyes again. This time it was easier. The light didn't seem quite so bright. There was a hazy form far overhead. Something tried to tell him to bring it into focus. The effort to do so hurt. He closed his eyes again. He touched his head. The pain seared through his mind jerking it back nearer to reality. He opened his eyes again. The form blurred then changed, came sharply into focus for a moment then blurred once more. Slim closed his eyes and opened them almost immediately. The roof of the stable was sharp and clear. He moved with an effort and then suddenly realised where he was. With that realisation came the knowledge of what had happened.

In something of a panic he sat up quickly. His body cried out at the exertion and his mind spun. He held his head and gradually he got his senses under control. As he took his hands from his head he was aware of the form lying near him. Chuck! This propelled Slim into action in spite of his pounding head. He pushed himself on to his knees and bent over the still form. There was a nasty cut around which the blood had congealed on Chuck's chin but Slim was relieved when he heard Chuck breathing.

Slim pushed himself to his feet, staggered, prevented himself from falling by grasping the woodwork of the stall, and moved on to find a bucket of water. He had spilled only a drop by the time he returned to Chuck. He slopped half the bucket over Chuck's face and the unconscious man stirred. Slim waited a moment then slopped more water over Chuck. This time he succeeded in reviving him. Chuck's eyes came open to focus quickly on Slim. His chin hurt. He felt it carefully. He winced with the pain.

'What happened?' he asked as he struggled to sit up.

'We were outsmarted by that bastard, Clinton,' said Slim.

The memory of the incident in the stable flooded back to Chuck. 'Hell! Red ain't going to like this,' he commented. He tried to stand up but needed Slim's assistance.

'He sure isn't,' agreed Slim, 'but we'll have to face him and the sooner the better.'

As soon as they felt they were able they left the stable by the single door and made their way to their horses.

Red Segal turned his horse away from the bunch of cattle which the Circle C men were handling. A movement, far across the range, had attracted him. He shielded his eyes against the glare of the mid-morning sun. His gaze beat through the distance. Two riders. Slim and Chuck? He could not tell from this distance but in anticipation of their arrival he stabbed his horse into a trot towards the two men.

He had covered about a quarter of a mile when he made a positive identification. Slim and Chuck. Eager to know that Clinton would trouble them no longer he kicked his mount into a gallop. His buoyant mood received a jolt when he saw the dejected way the two men were riding and he cursed inwardly when he saw the expressions on their faces. Something had gone wrong and they were not looking forward to reporting to Red.

'What went wrong this time?' he demanded harshly as he stopped to face his two men.

'He got to us first,' replied Chuck.

Red's eyes narrowed. Anger smouldered in them. 'Fools,' he rapped. 'Two of you should have been able to handle him without him knowing. What the hell happened?'

Slim and Chuck told the story between them, trying to make light of the matter, but Red was not fooled.

'Clinton was too smart for you.' His words were full of disgust and contempt for the two men. 'Wish I had him riding for me instead of you two dumbheads. If I read him right he won't be there when we get back, he's smart enough to figure I set him up. Easy pickings and you mess it up. Now he'll be harder to check on. I must know if he's riding with Matt Holbrook, so I want you to return to the Circle C by Holbrook's place, look it over to see if Clinton's there. But don't be seen if he is.'

'Want us to deal with him if he is?' asked Slim.

Red laughed with a touch of derision. 'What, let you make another mess and warn him we're still not finished with him?' He glared at the two men. 'Just find out if he's there.' He started to turn his horse but Slim stopped him.

'All right maybe we did slip up but we got news for you.' There was a note in Slim's voice which held a hope that what he was about to reveal would put them back in Red's good books.

'Well, spit it out,' snapped Red, irritated by Slim's hesitation.

'When we arrived at the stable we heard Buck and Chris having an argument. Seems Buck was set on Chris marrying Kathy Gibson and doesn't like Holbrook horning in. Buck saw the chance of making the Running W and Circle C the biggest spread in Montana being lost because Chris won't make a play for Kathy. I reckon from a remark Buck made he'd not stop at getting Holbrook out of the way.'

'I figured,' said Red thoughtfully. 'The hanging party that Clinton loused up would have done it.'

'You set that up,' said Slim. 'I thought this water supply business was the reason, but you figured...'

'Sure,' grinned Red. 'I reckon with no Holbrook Kathy would marry Chris. Buck ain't going to live for ever and who do you reckon would be running the big spread then?' A touch of wild ambition had come to his eyes.

'You!' Slim gasped as he realised the extent of Red's schemes.

'Sure. Too much responsibility for Chris, so Red Segal would be the real boss and coyotes like Clinton and Holbrook aren't going to mess it up.' His eyes narrowed as he looked hard at Slim and Chuck. 'Nor fools like you if you continue to slip up. Now git and see if you can get a line on Clinton without fouling it up.' He turned his horse sharply and sent it into a gallop towards the cattle which were being rounded up.

Slim and Chuck turned their mounts knowing that they would feel the wrath of Red if they did not carry out his orders successfully.

Planning to use any cover offered by the winding course of Elk River, the two men headed for its upper reaches, maintaining a steady pace across the grassland.

They dropped down into the small valley and turned their horses alongside the narrow water, thankful to find relief from the hot sun in the shade of the few small trees which grew near the water's edge. They moved slowly downstream, alert for any movement ahead.

Rounding a bend Slim, who was leading, pulled his mount to a halt and signalled Chuck to do the same. Martin's action was instantaneous for he too had seen the three wagons moving along the top of the rise on the opposite side of the river. He slid from the saddle, tied his horse to the branch of a tree and moved silently beside Slim who sat motionless on his horse.

'Figure them?' whispered Chuck.

'No,' he replied and continued to stare at the party on the opposite bank. 'Hold it. That's Holbrook, on the horse beside the first wagon.'

'Sure?' queried Chuck trying to beat his

gaze through the distance to verify the identification.

'Not certain, but it's rather like him.'

'I'll go back round the bend, cross the river and take a look at them as they pass,' whispered Chuck. 'You keep the horses here.'

Slim nodded his approval and Chuck moved silently away. Using the cover of the trees he followed the river until he could no longer see the wagons. He waded into the water and, though narrow, he found it deep enough to force him to swim a few yards in the middle. When he emerged on the opposite bank the wagons had still not come into sight so he lost no time in moving up the bank side to the cover of a small outcrop of rocks from which he would have a good view of the people with the wagons.

The wagons came slowly into view, rumbling and creaking their way along the top of the rise. Chuck watched them with deep intensity, he intended to have a detailed report for Red Segal, maybe he and Slim could get back into his favour. A man and woman rode on the first wagon, and Slim was right, the horseman riding alongside the lead wagon was Matt Holbrook! What was he doing with this party who looked as if they could be homesteaders?

As the first wagon moved nearer, revealing more of the second, Chuck saw that it was driven by a girl in her early twenties. Another girl rode a horse on the far side of this second wagon. She turned her head to speak to the girl on the wagon and a surprised excitement gripped Chuck when he recognised her. Kathy Gibson! Was she letting more people on to the Running W range? This was indeed news for Red Segal.

Kathy Gibson sent her horse forward to come alongside the driver of the first wagon. They were close to Chuck and he could hear her words distinctly as she called to the man who was driving.

'Another three miles, Mr Webster, you'll find this ridge dips a piece towards the river. I reckon that should be a good place to set up your home. Good access to the river and a bit of good land thereabouts.'

Webster smiled and nodded his thanks.

Homesteaders!

The word thundered in Chuck's mind. So he was right, these folks were homesteaders! This sure wouldn't please Buck Masters especially as they seemed to have the approval of the Gibsons.

Chuck watched the rest of the party go by. A young man drove the last wagon while another, whom Chuck reckoned was a brother, kept four horses moving steadily behind the wagon.

The earth powdered and billowed protestingly as the wagons rumbled on. Chuck waited until he reckoned any movement of his would go unnoticed before he moved down the bank, slipped into the water and crossed the river. Slapping some of the wet from himself he hurried back to Slim.

'Homesteaders!' he announced. 'And Holbrook and Kathy Gibson with them.'

Slim let out a slow whistle of surprise.

'Looks as though Gibson's backing them.'

'Sure does. I heard Kathy directing them to a site about three miles on.'

'Red's going to be mighty interested in this,' commented Slim. 'I figure we should keep our eye on them. They'll be plenty of time to check on Clinton after that.'

Chuck agreed and the two men turned their horses back along the river bank. They held well back, keeping the party on the opposite bank just comfortably in sight.

When the rise dipped and flattened towards the river in a two hundred yard stretch and the homesteaders directed their wagons nearer the river, Slim and Chuck halted their horses.

'Reckon we should take a closer look?' queried Slim.

Chuck nodded and the two men slid from the saddles, secured their mounts to a tree and moved cautiously along the bank using every available cover to avoid detection. They stopped among some bushes opposite to the wagons and watched the activity on the opposite side of the river.

Once the wagons had been positioned to Bill Webster's satisfaction, the horses were unhitched and all the animals were taken to the river to drink. Kemp brought some wood from one of the wagons and soon had a fire blazing. The women quickly set about preparing food and Matt, after exchanging a brief word with Kathy, came to Bill who was examining one of the horses at the river.

'He'll be all right, Ed,' Bill said with a smile at his son. He straightened and said to Matt, 'This sure is a nice place. We're mighty grateful for your help and of course to Miss Kathy for allowing us to stay here.' His words carried clearly across the narrow water to the two men hidden on the opposite bank.

Matt smiled. 'It's a good section of the country. Folks are friendly with exceptions, but not sure how they'll take to home-steaders. I reckon most will be all right when they know you have the approval of Wade Gibson, his word counts a lot around here.

But you might have trouble from the Circle C outfit. They're big and powerful, they figure I'm a threat to their water supply, might say the same for you if you're staying here.'

'Oh, we're staying. We're tired of moving on. We'll keep our eyes open for the Circle C. Thanks for the tip.'

FIVE

Slim figured they had heard all they needed to know. He tapped Chuck on the shoulder and with an inclination of his head indicated that he reckoned it was time for them to leave.

The two men crept quietly away and once they were sure it was safe to do so they rose to their feet and, using the cover of the trees, hurried quietly back to their horses.

'Looks as though that family's setting up for good,' commented Slim.

'Sure does,' agreed Chuck. 'Boss ain't going to like this.'

'Let's check on Clinton,' said Slim, 'then report to Red.'

They mounted their horses and, keeping close to the edge of the water and using it as a guide, headed for Matt Holbrook's place.

A short distance from it they left their horses tied to a tree and climbed the bank side to obtain a better view of the house. They lay waiting and watching and, although there was no movement, they sensed someone was about even though they knew Matt was with the homesteaders.

They had not long to wait before they got the information which confirmed Red Segal's suspicions. Johnny appeared and sat down on the veranda steps. The two men exchanged glances and then crept away to their horses which they led further from the water. Once they had climbed the bank they put their animals into a fast pace across the grassland.

Red Segal saw the tell-tale dust cloud before he saw the riders but once he had identified them he rode quickly in their direction. As the three men pulled their mounts to a halt, Red saw by the eagerness in their faces that Slim and Chuck had carried out their task successfully.

'He's at Holbrook's place?' Red's question

was partially a statement anticipating the answer.

'Yes,' replied Slim. 'But that ain't all.'

Red looked at Slim with a puzzled curiosity. He had received the information he had expected. Matt Holbrook and Johnny Clinton were riding together. What else could there be?

'Homesteaders!' Slim's announcement was so unexpected that for a moment there was no reaction from Red.

Then one word suddenly exploded from the Circle C foreman. 'What!' He stared at Slim hardly able to believe his ears. 'At Holbrook's place?' His question demanded the full story.

Slim and Chuck between them gave all the details to him.

'The boss is going to be mighty interested in this,' commented Red thoughtfully when he had heard the whole story. 'You go give a hand with the cattle, I'll go and see the boss.' As the two men moved away across the grassland towards the rising dust cloud,

Red turned his horse in the direction of the Circle C.

Once the Websters had settled Matt signalled to Kathy that he wanted to be going. They said their goodbyes and with homesteader thanks still in their ears they headed for Matt's place.

'Johnny was soon back from the Circle C,' commented Kathy, the first time she had been able to mention the subject to Matt since her arrival at his house earlier in the day.

'Yes, I didn't expect to see him back so soon but Segal rumbled him, that's all Johnny was able to tell me with the homesteaders about. I'm anxious to know what happened.'

Once on top of the rise above the river Kathy and Matt put their horses into a brisk pace. When they reached the house they found Johnny sitting on the veranda awaiting their return. As they pulled their horses to a halt in front of the house Johnny rose to his feet and held Kathy's horse while she dismounted.

'Get the Websters fixed up?' Johnny asked.

'Yes,' replied Kathy.

'You figure they'll be all right?' queried Johnny. 'The Circle C might cut up rough.'

'I warned them,' put in Matt, 'but they are tired of moving on and, getting a friendly reception from Kathy, they are determined to stay. But now, Johnny, what happened at the Circle C?'

Johnny shot a hard meaningful look at Matt and then glanced at Kathy. Matt got the message but before he could say anything Kathy put in a word.

'It's all right, Johnny, there's no need for me to be out of the way. This problem concerns me as much as it does Matt so speak up I want to know everything.'

Johnny grinned with embarrassment that Kathy had realised his meaning behind the unspoken message to Matt. He went on to tell them about what he had overheard and of his encounter with Slim and Chuck. 'I can't be sure whether they came gunning for me of their own accord after what happened in the saloon or whether Red sent them after me. I think that Red sent them otherwise they would be missed from the party that rode off from the Circle C.'

'I figure you've about hit the mark. You did right to come back,' said Matt. He turned to Kathy. 'Seems you and me are the real reason for the troubles. I'm sorry. Was there anything between you and Chris Masters before I came along?'

'It wouldn't matter if there was,' said Kathy. 'But there wasn't. Oh we are very good friends, after all we've been brought up together and seen a lot of each other. I suppose a lot of people think it would be the natural thing for us to marry. Maybe we would have if you hadn't come along, Matt.'

'Look, Kathy, if you and Chris…'

Kathy stopped him. 'It's you I love and it's you I'm going to marry, so that's an end to it.' There was a positive determination in her voice and Matt had the answer he had hoped for.

'Kathy, you know Buck Masters better than either of us, do you reckon he could be party to that hanging attempt yesterday?' asked Johnny.

'That's something that bothered me,' replied Kathy. 'Buck Masters is a hard man, I can see him trying to drive Matt away, using the water supply as an excuse but to go to the lengths of a hanging – I don't think so.'

Johnny nodded, looking thoughtful as he toyed with Kathy's opinion.

'What are you getting at?' asked Matt.

'Could someone else be behind it using Buck's attitude as a cover?' replied Johnny.

'That's elaborate,' said Matt.

'Not when the stakes are high,' Johnny pointed out.

'The two ranches,' whispered Kathy, incredulous that there could be someone with designs on the Circle C and the Running W.

'Right,' agreed Johnny.

'But that points to Buck,' Matt put in.

'You overheard that, Johnny.'

'Sure but not necessarily only Buck. Some-one could know of his ideas and be riding him along until the time is right to move against him.'

'But who?' queried Matt.

'If we knew that our troubles would be over,' said Kathy.

'What about Red Segal?' Johnny sug-gested.

'Segal?' Both Kathy and Matt were sur-prised at this suggestion.

'Yeah, why not?'

'But how can he gain out of it?' asked Kathy.

'I've been doing some thinking while you were away with the homesteaders,' replied Johnny, 'trying to figure out what gives. I reckoned like you, Kathy, that although Buck Masters is a hard man he would draw the line at a hanging. I gathered from what I over-heard that you and Chris think a lot about each other so I got to thinking what would happen if Matt was eliminated.' Johnny paused letting the meaning of his words sink in.

'I guess in all probability Chris and I would marry,' said Kathy quietly.

At this announcement words started to rush to Matt's lips but Johnny stopped him.

'Don't go flying off, Matt, that is only a possibility. You here makes a difference. Right, suppose the situation of Kathy marrying Chris arises then Buck has achieved his aim and when Kathy's father dies the two ranches become one and Buck runs them.'

'Not with me around,' said Kathy indignantly.

'That's another story,' said Johnny, 'and I guess certain folks would find they'd underestimated Chris.'

'I think you're right. Chris is not as hard as his father, not as ruthless,' agreed Kathy. 'His father rules him at the Circle C, won't let him have a say in the running of the ranch but in a different situation I reckon Chris would give some people a surprise.'

'Right,' went on Johnny. 'And one of those

people could be Red Segal.'

'You mean, once Kathy and Chris were married and the two ranches became one he'd get rid of Buck figuring that he'd rule the spread because he figures Chris wouldn't be capable of it.' Matt was amazed at the idea.

'Something like that,' Johnny replied. 'He could milk off a lot of money ruling the biggest spread in Montana.'

'It's going to take some proving,' Matt pointed out.

'Dare say but at least this guesswork gives us something to go on. If Kathy had said that Buck was capable of arranging a hanging party that would have been a different matter.'

'What can we do about it?' asked Kathy.

'If only you had still been on the inside, Johnny. A pity Red rumbled you.' Matt looked troubled as he tried to think of some solution to their problem.

'I reckon for the moment we'll just have to let things take their course and be ready to seize any chance that comes up. One thing's for sure, Red Segal won't sit quiet,' said Johnny.

'Nor will Buck Masters,' added Kathy, 'especially when he hears about the Websters.'

Red Segal arrived at the Circle C and went straight into the house to find Buck working at his desk.

Surprised by the unexpected intrusion the rancher looked up. 'What brings you back?' Buck's tone was harsh still reflecting the irritation he felt at the disagreement with his son.

Red did not mince matters. 'Homesteaders!'

Buck stared at him incredulously for a moment as the word numbed his brain and then made its impact. 'What!'

'It's right. Slim and Chuck saw them.'

'Where?' Buck had jumped to his feet.

'Other side of Elk River. Upstream from Holbrook. Kathy Gibson was with them, seems she showed them where to pitch camp.'

'Staying?'

'Sounded like it from what Slim and Chuck overheard.'

'Like hell they are. Holbrook was bad enough but at least he is running cattle. But homesteaders – I'll see what Wade has to say about this. His daughter can't go around letting in who she likes.' He grabbed his Stetson and hurried towards the door.

'Want me along, boss?' Red asked.

'No. I'll handle this,' Buck called over his shoulder.

Red smiled to himself when he heard the outside door close. He sat on the corner of the desk, selected a cigar from a box which stood at one corner, lit it carefully and drew on it long and deep. He let the smoke out slowly, then walked round to the chair behind the desk and sat down. Some day this would be the way, he would be giving orders from this side of the desk instead of taking them at the other.

Buck saddled his horse quickly and left the Circle C at a fast gallop. The pace matched his temper all the way to the Running W. He was out of the saddle almost before the horse had stopped in front of the ranch-house. He flung the reins over the hitching rail, climbed the four steps in two strides and went into the house.

Buck knew where to find Wade and went to the second door on the right. His big frame burst straight into the room without even the courtesy of a knock on the woodwork. The pale-faced man, whose illness had emaciated a once well-filled frame, looked startled by the sudden intrusion. He regained his composure quickly when he recognised the blustering temperament of Buck Masters, something which he had become used to during their twenty years as neighbours.

'What the hell's the idea letting home-steaders settle up Elk River?' Buck demanded as he glared down at Wade who shuffled to settle himself more comfortably in his chair.

'Homesteaders!' Wade was taken aback by Buck's unexpected information. 'I know nothing about them, first I've heard.'

'They're on your land, upstream from Holbrook. Two of my men saw them. And, Wade, Kathy was with them showing them where to put down their roots.'

'If Kathy knows about it then it will be all right,' countered Wade.

'Like hell it will,' boomed Buck. 'They may be on your land but you know as well as I do that let one homesteader family settle and there'll be others.'

'Not necessarily,' said Wade.

'More than likely. Others come along see a family settled, figure there's a friendly cattleman around so do the same. Before you know where we are there'll be the makings of a town. It'll be sitting astride the river, vital for our water supply.'

'Better wait and see what Kathy has to say. I won't be here to see those problems if they arise, they'll be her affair.'

'Don't know how you can take it so lightly,' commented Buck irritably. 'If she was my daughter I'd want to see her married to someone who knew the cattle business.'

Wade stiffened. He glared at Buck. 'She knows it,' he rasped.

'Sure, but there are times when you need a man about the place, times like this when homesteaders should be moved on and not encouraged to stay. Don't know why you don't press her to marry Chris. The two spreads together would be powerful enough to resist anyone.'

'I know, Buck, there was a day, when we were all younger, when we thought and probably hoped that the friendship between Kathy and Chris would blossom into marriage but it's up to the youngsters themselves. Seems they never thought that way, at least not that we know of, and then comes along Matt Holbrook.'

'That two-bit rancher should never have been allowed to settle.'

'The youngster wanted to be given a

chance, there's no harm in that.'

'He's right next to the river.'

'Water supply troubling you again, Buck,' said Wade with a wry smile. 'You've blustered about that before. Wouldn't be worth Holbrook's time trying to interfere with our water supply, we could easily deal with him. Maybe you saw him winning Kathy's affections, well, that's happened so leave it, Buck. Don't meddle in things which don't concern you, don't use the water as an excuse to move Holbrook on.' Wade's voice and eyes had gone cold. His meaning was not lost on Buck and the owner of the Circle C knew that even though Wade was a sick man he could still be a tough one.

The argument was cut short when the door opened and Kathy walked in. She immediately recognised an agitation in her father and knowing it wasn't good for him to get worked up she hurried to his side.

'You all right, pa?' she asked, concern showing on her face.

'Sure, honey,' Wade smiled and patted her

hand reassuringly.

She glanced at Buck but before she could say anything he directed words at her father.

'Go on Wade, ask her about the home-steaders.'

Kathy straightened and smiled. 'So you know about them.'

'Two of my men, Slim Taylor and Chuck Martin saw them, and you with them. What the hell's the idea of giving them a place to settle?'

Kathy's mind gasped at the names. They may be Circle C riders but they were also Red Segal's sidekicks. 'The Websters were tired of being moved on–'

'So you took pity on them,' cut in Buck scornfully.

'If you like,' retorted Kathy. 'They seemed nice folk and that land up there was of no importance so I figured it might be put to good use.'

'Never stopped to think that it could lead to other folks homesteading there and before long we could have the makings of a town.'

Kathy smiled. 'Well it just so happens that I did. Your two riders couldn't have stayed long enough to hear me tell them that I was letting one family and one family only settle, that if others came they'd have to move on.'

Wade grinned up at his neighbour. 'That satisfy you, Buck. I told you Kathy was capable.'

Buck glared at them. 'We'll see how it turns out,' he grunted and swung on his heel and stormed out of the house.

As the door banged behind Masters Wade laughed. 'Poor old Buck, gets riled quickly.'

'Sure, but I wish he wouldn't come over here worrying you about it. See, if he'd checked with me first there'd have been no need for you to get all worked up.'

'Don't worry. I'm all right.'

Kathy's face went serious and Wade knew from experience that something was troubling her and she wanted advice but the question was not forthcoming, instead Kathy started to walk towards the door.

SIX

'Kathy.' Wade's voice, quiet but firm, halted his daughter. She turned to him. 'There's something wrong,' he continued, 'something troubling you. Once you would have come to me and talked it out. What's wrong with now?'

'It's nothing, Pa. Really it isn't.'

'You don't convince me, Kathy. I know you only too well. I may not have long to live, I'm not physically active like I used to be, so please let me share your problems, let me be useful in this way like I've always been.'

Kathy looked hard at her father for a moment then realised she was taking something away from him by not sharing the problems like she used to do. She walked slowly back to him, dropped on her knees beside his chair and took his hands in hers.

'I'm sorry, Pa. I didn't want to worry you.'

Wade smiled. 'Worry? I'm here to help, to share your problems.'

'Thanks.'

'Now what is it all about?'

'Do you think Buck Masters is capable of organising a hanging party?'

Wade was startled by the question. 'Buck, a hanging party?'

'Yes, if someone stole a horse.'

'There's rough justice with horse thieves but, as tough and as rough as Buck can be, I figure that nowadays he'd draw the line at hanging. In the old days when he and I were trying to battle with this land, maybe, but not now. But why? What brought this about?'

'The other day Matt nearly felt a rope round his neck.'

'What?'

'There was a Circle C horse in his corral and some of the Circle C outfit were about to hang him when this fella, Johnny Clinton, appeared and saved him. Matt said the horse had been planted.'

'So he figures it was used to get him out of the way.'

'Yes. Do you think Buck could be behind it?'

'No!' The word came swift and convincing.

'I'm glad to hear you say that,' Kathy smiled and her father could see the relief which came over his daughter.

'You were afraid I might think he was and afraid of what that might mean,' said Wade gently. 'Buck wouldn't go round planting horses. If he wanted someone out of the way he'd come straight out with it and tell them to git and he wouldn't take no for an answer, but his actions would all be in the open. He blustered when Matt first came, just as he's blustering now that you've let some home-steaders in, but so long as they keep to our side of the river and don't give him cause to come and say I told you so then he'll take no action.'

'That bears out Johnny's theory,' Kathy smiled.

'Johnny's theory?'

Kathy told her father all that had happened and how Johnny had put forward an idea that Red Segal might be playing for big stakes.

Wade was thoughtful for a few moments after Kathy had finished her story, then, a wry smile on his lips, he looked at his daughter. 'It would have saved a lot of bother if you had married Chris.'

'Pa, I...' Kathy started to protest as she scrambled to her feet.

'I know, I know,' cut in Wade. 'I'm not saying you should do so.'

'Maybe you would have liked me to,' said Kathy.

'I won't deny that at one time I was like Buck and hoped you and Chris might marry and unite the ranches but I soon realised that after Matt had come on the scene he had captured your heart. As for that incident between Chris and his father that Johnny overheard when Chris said Buck wanted to rule the biggest spread in Montana, well I figure that was just Chris shooting off in the heat of the moment. I don't figure Buck wanted that. But Johnny's theory about Red Segal is another matter. I'd like to meet this here Johnny Clinton. Sometimes outsiders bring a fresh viewpoint which someone close to the situation overlooks. He could be right.'

'Well you'll have the opportunity to meet him this evening. I've asked him and the homesteaders over so you can meet them.'

Red Segal was watching for Buck's return and he sought the owner of the Circle C shortly after he had gone into the ranch-house.

'Make anything out, boss?' Red asked.

'Told Wade what I thought but he wouldn't go against what Kathy had done, and she had me because she's said one family and one only.' His eyes narrowed in the annoyance he was feeling. 'But just let one of those homesteaders step out of line and they'll be moving on.'

'I'll post someone to keep an eye on them,' said Red.

A few minutes later when he left the house he smiled to himself. He'd keep tabs on the homesteaders all right but it would be for his own ends not those of Buck Masters.

Red rode out to the men with the cattle and called Slim and Chuck to one side.

'I want you back at Elk River,' he told them, 'keeping an eye on the homesteaders. One wrong move and we move 'em on.'

'Or make them feel they'd be better off elsewhere?' grinned Chuck.

'Could be,' returned Red. 'But they're not to know it's you.'

The two men nodded and sent their horses away with a sharp tap on the side with their heels.

They came to the river between Matt's house and the homesteaders' camp and made their way through the trees until they were able to take up a good position from which to keep the camp in sight.

It was early evening when Slim shook

Chuck who was dozing. 'Things happening,' he whispered. 'The Websters have been sprucing themselves up and now they're hitching the horses to the wagon which they emptied during the afternoon.'

The two men watched until they had seen all the family pile into the wagon and Bill Webster pick up the reins and drive away.

'Reckon we'll follow,' said Slim.

They slipped through the trees to their horses tethered a short distance away. They crossed the river and, with only a casual glance at the camp, moved on to the grassland. They followed the creaking, rumbling wagon for a couple of miles before Slim halted his horse.

'I figure they're heading for the Running W.'

Chuck agreed. 'Reckon they must have had an invite from Miss Kathy.'

'To meet her pa most likely,' said Slim. As he watched the wagon growing smaller a grin spread across his face. 'We might just take the opportunity of letting them know they're not wanted around. Let you and I go and have a little fun.'

Chuck grinned as Slim's meaning came to him. They turned their horses and rode back towards Elk River and the homesteaders' camp.

The evening had passed off well and Kathy had soon realised that the homesteaders were making a good impression on her father.

'We've sure enjoyed this evening,' said Bill Webster as he shook hands with Wade. 'Thanks for your hospitality.'

'Pleasure's mine,' returned Wade with a smile. 'I approve of Kathy's decision but I must emphasise what she said about one family only. I've got my fellow cattlemen to think about and they wouldn't want to see me encouraging more homesteaders, frightened of what it might lead to.'

'You have my assurance on this,' replied Bill. 'We won't attract anyone else.'

'Good,' said Wade. 'Another thing, I'll

keep you supplied with meat but you'll have to wait for the first lot until we've done some checking at branding time which will be soon.'

Bill made his thanks and said his good-byes. Whilst he was doing so Wade caught the attention of Johnny. 'Young fella, I'd like to have a talk with you, come and see me tomorrow.'

As Wade offered no explanation Johnny left the Running W in a puzzled frame of mind. He was quiet and thoughtful as he and Matt accompanied the Websters back to their camp.

As they dipped over the rise on to the slope to the river Bill tugged on the reins and pulled the horses drawing the wagon to a halt. He stared in numbed amazement at the chaos in the camp.

'Bill!' His wife's gasping cry really demanded an answer to his own unspoken questions of Who? and Why?

'Hold it right there Mr Webster,' called Johnny. He tapped his horse's side with his

95

heels and the animal moved forward. Johnny kept it to a walking pace as every muscle in his body tensed into alertness ready for instant action. His eyes searched and probed trying to pick up any sign of human presence. Whoever had wrecked the camp might still be around awaiting the opportunity to take the homesteaders while their attention was occupied with the chaos.

He rode through the scattered personal belongings of the Webster family, past the food ground into the earth, and viewed the overturned wagon as a possible cover for the intruders. When he was satisfied there was no one about he continued down the slope to the river. He halted his horse at the water's edge and stared across the water. Nothing stirred in the stillness. The darkness intensified along the river bank where the moonlight failed to penetrate the trees. Johnny was suspicious. He tapped his mount and put it cautiously into the water. He moved across the ford slowly, his eyes constantly on the move, straining in their search.

Water marked the ground as the horse came out of the river. Johnny eased it to a halt. He sat still, trying to catch any sound above the noise of the flowing water at his back. His heels touched horseflesh and the animal stepped forward. It was a moment in time that saved Johnny's life for, at the very second that he made the decision to move, a finger squeezed a trigger. A rifle crashed from among the trees to Johnny's right and the bullet whistled uncomfortably close to his head.

Johnny left the saddle so fast that his would-be assassin saw only empty space even as he squeezed the trigger for a second shot. The blast of the rifle scared Johnny's horse. It spun round and crashed its way across the ford in a great welter of water.

The ground came hard at Johnny but in the instant of escaping from death he relaxed and took the contact without any effect. He rolled over quickly tugging at his Colt as he came over on to his stomach. He loosed off two shots in the general direction from which the bullets had come, then rolled over twice. A crashing noise came from the trees, Johnny distinguishing it from the pound of hooves from across the river.

The sound of the first shot and the sight of the blurred figure of Johnny falling from the saddle brought an instant instinctive reaction from the watchers on the other side of the river. Lydia's cry showed that she feared that they had seen the last of Johnny alive, while the three youngsters stared in bewilderment, each locked with their own thoughts about the man of whom they knew so little yet who had protected them by disclosing the presence of a killer with his own life. That shots came from the ground close to where Johnny had fallen did not register emphatically enough to form a positive impression through their anxiety.

Bill Webster's immediate need was to get to Johnny as quickly as possible and with a yell he sent his team of two heading for the river. Unencumbered by a wagon, Matt was way ahead of the Websters. The sound of the rifle was still echoing from the trees when Matt dug his heels hard into his horse and sent it without consideration into an earth-pounding gallop to the river.

Oblivious to his own safety, ignoring the fact that even now the killer might be drawing a line on him, Matt stormed across the river. With his mind set on one thing, reaching Johnny, Matt was not aware of other sounds which had broken out among the trees. The shots which Johnny had fired had registered in Matt's subconscious and, as he pulled hard on the reins, he knew Johnny was alive. Matt swung from the saddle before the animal had stopped and as he dropped beside Johnny the animal, freed of its burden, gradually slowed its run.

'You all right?' Matt panted his question as he drew air into his lungs, heaving after the sudden exertion.

'Sure,' replied Johnny. 'Listen.'

Matt inclined his head and above the rumble of Webster's wagon and the gurgle of the flowing water he heard the sound of galloping horses heading away from the trees.

'Two of them,' said Johnny as he scrambled to his feet.

Bill Webster hauled hard to stop the wagon beside the water and with a yell of 'Stay here!' to his family he threw the reins to his eldest son and jumped from the seat. He sent water spraying around him as he ran across the ford.

'Johnny!' The word was gasped from Bill's heaving chest.

Johnny holstered his Colt and turned to reassure Bill that he was all right. 'Two of them,' he said indicating the sound of galloping horses which was receding with every hoof beat.

'Circle C bastards, I'll bet,' hissed Bill. 'Lend me your horse, Matt.' He started towards the animal which was wandering slowly back towards them.

Johnny grasped Bill's arm, restraining him. 'Forget it,' he said. 'No doubt you're right but you can't prove anything. You'll just ride into one heap of trouble.'

'Circle C wants us out.' Bill's lips were set in a tight line, his eyes smouldered with a dark anger.

'Sure,' agreed Johnny. 'From what I saw as I rode through your camp only the food is a total loss, the rest'll take some tidying up. They could have fired the lot and gunned you down, so I reckon this is just a warning to move on.'

'But someone took a shot at you, you figure that was just a warning?' said Bill.

'No, that bullet was meant to kill. Lucky for me I moved when I did. I figured that whoever had been at your camp might stay to watch your reactions and if it was the Circle C they'd do it from their side of the river. That's why I crossed, to test them out.'

'You were taking a risk,' said Matt.

'Reckon so, but I figure it's given us a good idea who it was. Slim and Chuck.'

'You figure they seized the opportunity to take revenge, if it had been anyone else they wouldn't have fired?'

'Something like that,' agreed Johnny.

'Gave themselves away, you reckon?' he nodded with a grin.

The three men returned to the camp where the rest of the family were delighted to learn that Johnny was all right.

The anxious tension which had gripped Lydia drained from her and was replaced by despair as she surveyed the camp.

'Oh, Bill, are we right in staying?' she cried as the tears welled in her eyes. 'Is it going to be the same all over again?' Heightened by the delayed shock the tears flowed.

Bill put a comforting arm around her shoulder. 'We aren't going anywhere. We've found friends so we're staying right here. This is going to be our home.' His words were gentle, reassuring, firmed with a fierce determination. He looked up. His voice boomed. 'Ed, Kemp, Rhona, let's get our home set straight.'

The three young Websters, delighted by and approving of their father's determination to make a stand, raced off to start work. Johnny and Matt joined them and soon the camp was looking reasonable again.

'You'll have no food for the morning so come over to my place for breakfast and afterward someone can carry on into town for fresh supplies,' suggested Matt as he and Johnny were saying their goodbyes.

'Thanks. That's mighty nice of you,' said Lydia. 'Maybe Rhona could go to town; there'll be plenty for the men folk to do here.'

'We're grateful.' Bill added his thanks then turned to Johnny. 'And to you too. You risked your life, that's something which will live with us.'

Johnny looked hard at Bill. 'Just a word of advice. Don't go bucking any cattlemen; don't provoke them; don't give them a chance to hit back.'

Bill nodded, his mind toying with Johnny's words as he watched the two men ride away. What if the cattlemen hit first, just as they had tonight?

SEVEN

The following morning after breakfasting with Matt and Johnny, Rhona Webster prepared to go into Roundup to replace their lost supplies.

'You be all right with that team?' her mother queried.

'Of course, ma, you know I will. I've handled them before.'

'I'd come along but there's so much to do back at camp.' She kissed her daughter. 'You be careful now,' she added as she climbed on to the second wagon beside her husband.

Rhona watched them go then climbed on to the wagon she was taking to town. Johnny emerged from the stable leading his saddled horse.

'Wade Gibson wants to see me,' he called to Matt. 'Asked me to call this morning. I'll

go now then I can ride so far with Rhona.'
He swung into the saddle and with a nod to
Matt, put his horse alongside the wagon as
Rhona flicked the reins to send the horses
forward.

Johnny enjoyed the leisurely ride and the
pleasant conversation with only the creak of
leather and wood to interrupt. Four miles
from Matt's place Johnny took his leave and
headed across the grassland for the Running
W.

Rhona found Roundup busy with its daily
routine and had to curb the impatience of
her two horses as she waited for a wagon to
move from in front of the store. Once she
had made her purchases, the storeman's
assistant loaded the wagon for her. Several
people were attracted by the sight of a young
woman handling a wagon team as she drove
out of town but none more so than the man
who lounged on a chair outside the saloon.
After the wagon had passed he pushed himself from his chair and unhitched his horse
from the rail. He swung into the saddle and

rode in the opposite direction. He smiled to himself when he thought how last night, when pressed for a description of the homesteaders, Chuck Martin had described the desirability of this young woman. He turned down a side street and left town.

The noise of barking dogs in an alley did not worry Rhona as she neared the end of the main street. But her peaceful progress was suddenly erupted into a maelstrom of danger. A dog, with another snarling close at its heels, burst from the alley. Dust churned as its flight took it straight across the main street right at the wagon's horses. The pursuer's extra strength gained it those inches of separation and suddenly the horizontal streak of dogs became a rolling, whirling ball of fury. Snarling sounds of victory were mingled with cries of pain as the animals fought a vicious battle. Dust rose from the tumbling mass which crashed against the legs of the horses pulling Rhona's wagon.

Startled by the noisy intrusion the horses whinnied with fright and reared to try to get away from the fury beneath their feet. Rhona suddenly found herself battling to keep the horses under control and prevent them from tearing into a gallop. Held back they twisted and turned as much as their harness and shaft would allow. They needed to be away from the frightening thing which howled at their feet.

At almost the moment of triumph the victor slightly relaxed the intensity of its fight. The vanquished seized that moment for escape. It twisted and turned, broke from beneath the horses and ran headlong down the main street. No sooner was it away and the other dog was in pursuit.

But fear was still in the horses and they fought to be away from this spot. In her contest for control Rhona had stood up and now was in danger of being jerked from the wagon. Her face was lined in terror as the fear that she was not going to win gripped her. Though she fought strongly she felt weak and helpless against the power of the two horses.

Chris Masters came out of the bank into a whirl of noise of fighting dogs and whinnying horses. He sized up the situation in one glance and broke into a run for the wagon. He reached it as the dogs hurtled down the main street and he saw that the girl would succumb to the muscle-tearing pull of the horses. Without losing a second he was at the head of the animals, grasping at their leather and exerting his strength to control them. They jerked their heads trying to rid themselves of this new encumbrance but Chris fought them, all the time calling out to them in a soothing voice. This gentleness after the howling terror penetrated their brains and gradually they stopped their attempt to run. Even after they were still Chris remained at their heads speaking quietly and stroking them gently.

With a great sigh of relief Rhona let go of the reins and slumped on the seat. In the aftermath of fright and exertion she was shaking but she fought to take control of herself as a crowd gathered round the wagon.

People called out asking if she was all right but she was only aware of the help offered when Chris climbed on the wagon beside her.

'Are you all right?' he enquired gently.

Rhona could not find any words but she nodded as she fought back the tears.

'No harm done.' Chris called out and, knowing she would be better away from everybody's gaze he picked up the reins, called to the horses and sent them forward. The crowd began to break up and Chris walked the horses slowly to the edge of town. When he halted them he turned to Rhona.

'They should be all right now,' he said, 'but it might be better if you sat quietly for a few minutes.'

Rhona had regained most of her composure. 'Thank you for what you did. I couldn't have held them much longer.'

Chris smiled wanting to reassure her that all would be well. 'Nobody with you?' he asked.

'No,' replied Rhona. Seeing the surprised

look on Chris' face she added quickly. 'I'm used to handling a wagon team but today was a bit exceptional.'

'I'll say.' Chris smiled. 'You're sure you feel all right?'

'Yes thanks,' Rhona replied as she brushed back the unruly hair which fell across the side of her face.

'Have you far to go? Would you like me to ride along with you?'

'No there's no need for that,' replied Rhona. 'I can manage.'

'Very well,' Chris said. He glanced at the horses which were standing quite calmly. 'They should be no more trouble,' he added and handed the reins to Rhona. He jumped down from the wagon, turned and smiled at her.

'Thanks again,' she said and with a shake of the reins sent the team on its way out of Roundup.

Chris stood watching the wagon wondering about the girl whose prettiness and courage had made an impression on him.

He turned and walked slowly to the livery stable. He had almost reached the building when he realised the girl had not told him where she was going and that they had not exchanged names. Well, maybe he would run into her again in town.

After collecting his horse, Chris took it to the blacksmiths, made two other calls and half an hour later rode out of Roundup. There was no hurry and as he kept to a gentle pace his mind drifted to the girl on the wagon.

Topping a rise in the trail Chris pulled his horse to a halt. The wagon! A chance to meet the girl again! He was about to heel his horse after the rumbling vehicle when his attention was drawn to a rider galloping at a tangent to the trail which on Chris' estimation would bring him behind the wagon. There seemed to be an urgency about the pace of the rider. Chris frowned. Trouble? A message? He held his horse still and watched.

The horseman was so intent on reaching the wagon that he failed to notice the rider on top of the rise. He kept his horse to its fast pace, swung on to the trail and rapidly closed the distance to the wagon.

Rhona was not aware of the thundering hoofbeats until they were close. Curious, she glanced back round the side of the wagon and was surprised to see a rider intent on overtaking her. She half checked the team but then she saw the look on the rider's face. Evil stalked from the eyes anticipating the pleasure to come. There was no mistaking the rider's intention. Fingers of cold fear closed round Rhona's being. They seemed to freeze her into immobility, lengthening the moments into hours of horror. In fact it was only a second before she was round on the seat urging and lashing at the horses. Startled by the suddenness of demand they leapt forward and charged into a gallop.

But it was too late. The rider was alongside the rear of the wagon. He reached out, grasped the metal canvas support, kicked his feet loose of the stirrups, steadied himself then, taking the strain on his arms, heaved himself from the saddle and swung round into the wagon. He crashed among the purchases from the store, bringing a startled scream from Rhona. She looked round, her eyes widening with terror when she saw the man scrambling to his feet. He steadied himself against the sway of the wagon and advanced towards her.

Chris had watched the scene with an intense interest, unsure of the rider's motives. But when he saw the wagon team break into a gallop he knew the rider was no messenger but spelt trouble with a capital T. Chris kicked his horse forward sending it into an earth-tearing speed along the trail. When he saw the man swing into the wagon Chris wished he had anticipated the worst and moved sooner. There was not a moment to waste.

Knowing that a short distance ahead the trail made a long curve to the right, Chris turned his horse across the grassland and urged it to greater speed. The animal responded and its hooves tore at the ground driving it faster and faster. Chris judged his line across the grassland in relation to the trail and with a firm but gentle indication eased his horse so that it would reach the trail sooner and if his estimation was correct a little ahead of the wagon.

The seat of the wagon was in Chris' view and his inside tensed when he saw the girl turn towards the inside of the wagon and strike out. The next instant she was gone, dragged inside by powerful hands. Chris yelled to his horse. The hooves pounded at the anxiety thrumming in his brain. It seemed he would never out ride the wagon dragged by horses now out of control.

As the distance shortened the angle closed rapidly and then Chris was racing alongside the stretching, straining team. A quick glance at the wagon told him that his arrival had gone unnoticed. He had an advantage. Now it all depended how quickly he could bring the horses under control. Once there was an alteration in their pace the assailant in the wagon would know there was an outside influence on the animals.

Chris brought his horse nearer and nearer to the team. They were in full flight with the wagon clattering and swaying behind them. He was close to the right-hand horse with its mane flying and its neck stretched forward. He edged his mount closer. Hooves pounded in a terrifying beat. Chris realised that one slight error could see him dragged under the flaying feet of the frightened horses.

He measured his distance carefully, drew his animal in closer, concentrated his mind on the harness then suddenly he leaned from the saddle and grabbed the leather. It felt as if his left arm was being dragged from his body which cried for him to let go. He held on and at the same time kept control of his own horse. For a few brief moments they galloped on as one then Chris began to exert a pressure, pulling back, slowing his own mount, matching it to the decrease in speed of the team. The safest thing would have been to slow the animals gradually but there was not time. He threw all caution aside, for his broad back was exposed to the man in the wagon and any moment a shot might take him.

Dragged from her seat and hurled back against a sack Rhona cried out as pain shot through her body. She slid to the floor of the wagon trying to regain the air which had been forced from her lungs by the impact. Her eyes were wide with terror as she looked up at the man stepping towards her, bracing his body against the sway of the wagon. An ugly scar flamed down his left cheek adding to the horrific look which filled the darkness of his face. His eyes were fired with a deep lust and his lips were parted in a leering grin of satisfaction.

He leaned forward and reached out with a massive, hairy hand. Rhona cringed, trying to push herself further away from the menace which closed in on her. The blood pounded in her brain. She screamed. He laughed at her natural reaction to attract attention. His hand closed round the front of her dress. He paused a moment looking deep in her eyes, savouring the effect he was having on her. She screamed again. He pulled hard ripping the dress from her right shoulder to her waist. He grinned with pleasure as he gripped both her shoulders and pulled her to her feet. He hesitated for a moment again while he looked hard at her. She twisted her head from side to side as he lowered his mouth towards hers. Suddenly he straightened and flung her across two sacks leaning against the side of the wagon. The breath was once more driven from her body but in spite of this she struggled to get up. Suddenly a huge hand clamped her below the throat, pinning her down while his other hand sought to rip her dress from her body. Rhona struggled, fighting her attacker as well as the feeling of utter hopelessness which swept over her.

She brought her knees up sharply, catching him in the side. Her hand reached up, clawing at his face and tearing at the arm which held her down. She kneed him again.

The sharpness of the blow coupled with a vicious swaying of the wagon caused her attacker to momentarily ease his grip. Rhona twisted and slid from the sacks but he held on. He yanked her to her feet again. In her desperate fight Rhona found new strength. She pummelled at his face with clenched fists. It warded him off for a few moments before he brought his open hand hard across her face. She staggered backwards and fell against some boxes. The strength drained from her body. She felt helpless. He moved towards her, his dark eyes bored into her. He had come to take her and take her he would. There was nothing she could do.

He reached down. Rhona pushed herself away wanting to avoid the awful touch, but boxes resisted her effort. The leering face came closer.

Suddenly her attacker froze. His expression changed to one of annoyed puzzlement. The wagon was slowing! What was happening outside? Someone interfering? He swung round, tense, ready to release himself. The wagon slowed more. It swayed precariously sending him hard against the side canvas. He cursed as he shoved himself to his feet. The wagon would soon be at a standstill. Someone must be stopping it, the horses would not have slowed this way of their own accord. He clawed at his gun.

With the first slowing of the wagon Rhona's hopes of rescue soared. When her attacker turned away from her it brought a relief and a new determination to her. She started to push herself to her feet but fell back as the wagon swayed. She heard her attacker curse and when she saw him drawing his Colt she found some hidden reserves of strength. He was facing the front of the wagon, she must do something, he must not shoot whoever was out there, her only hope of rescue.

Gasping, she struggled to her feet. He stepped forward, pushed the loose canvas aside so that he could see out without being seen. He raised his Colt. The wagon stopped. Rhona, her face twisted in the anguish of desperation, launched herself at the broad back. The impact, though not strong, was sufficient to throw him off balance and send him through the canvas to sprawl against the wagon's seat.

Relieved when the team came to a halt, Chris whirled his own horse round so as not to present an easy target. The expected shot never came. As he turned he saw the girl's attacker stumble through the loose canvas and fall. Chris' hand closed round the butt of his Colt and in the same movement slid the gun from its leather. The canvas parted again and the girl, breathing heavily from exertion, clawed at her attacker trying to stop him from bringing his gun to bear on her rescuer.

'Hold it!' Chris' voice demanded instant obedience.

The girl stopped her struggle and with relief showing on her face straightened only to become embarrassed by her torn and dishevelled appearance and disappeared into the wagon.

The man on the wagon pushed himself up, dropping his gun in surrender as he did so. His face revealed his surprise on seeing Chris.

Chris was equally taken aback. 'Blackie!' he gasped, his eyes darkening with anger. 'what the hell...?' His gun was menacing. Blackie licked his lips nervously. He didn't think Chris would shoot but who could tell when a girl was concerned. The tension of the second seemed to drift on. 'Get to hell out of here!' rapped Chris. 'Collect your things from the ranch and disappear, 'cos if I come across you again you'll get what you deserve!'

Blackie hesitated a moment as he glared at Chris but he thought better of trying to outwit him. He jumped down from the wagon and without a word set off across the grassland to his horse which had stopped a short distance away.

Chris watched him go, holstered his gun then swung from the saddle and led his horse to the back of the wagon to which he secured it on a long rein. As he reached the front of the wagon again, the canvas parted and the girl, her torn dress secured as best she could, came out.

'You all right?' asked Chris gently as he climbed on to the seat.

She flopped down beside him and looked hard at him for a moment then the feelings of revulsion at the attack and relief at her rescue could not be contained. The tears flowed unashamedly and Chris took her in his arms and let her cry the trouble out of herself.

Once that tension had flowed from her, Rhona took a grip on her feelings. She pushed herself out of Chris' arms and as she wiped the tears from her eyes looked apologetically at him.

'I'm sorry,' she whispered.

'You have nothing to be sorry for after what you have been through,' said Chris soothingly.

'Do you know who he was?' Rhona queried.

Chris was relieved to learn from her question that she had not overheard what had passed between himself and Blackie. 'He's from one of the ranches around here,' replied Chris vaguely.

'Circle C I suppose,' said Rhona bitterly.

Chris was surprised at her statement. 'What makes you say that?' he asked.

'We've had trouble with them already,' she said.

'In what way?'

'They raided our camp.' Rhona went on to relate the happenings of the previous night. 'If the Running W can accept us why can't the Circle C? We're doing them no harm, we're on Wade Gibson's land.' She posed her concern after concluding her story.

Chris' mind was awhirl with her revelations. Things were happening that he didn't know about. His father had been antagonistic towards Matt Holbrook when he first settled beside Elk River but that feeling had been tempered over recent weeks. Now another family was beside the river had his old feeling flared up again? Had he organised the raid as a warning and had Blackie interpreted the antagonism to mean get rid of the homesteaders at any price? Chris was puzzled for he had not heard his father mention the homesteaders but then he and his father were not on the best of terms at the moment.

Chris shrugged his shoulders. 'I don't know,' he answered, then quickly changed the subject while resolving to have the matter out with his father. 'I reckon when I offer to escort you back to your camp you'd better accept this time. A pity you didn't when we were in town.'

Rhona smiled. 'I guess I should have done but I do now. We've been talking all this time and I don't even know who to thank for saving me.'

'Chris,' he replied avoiding his surname as he didn't want associating with the Circle C.

She nodded. 'And call me Rhona.'

Chris gathered up the reins and set the

wagon in motion. The pleasant ride and Chris' presence had a calming effect on Rhona and by the time the encampment was in sight she was herself again. Her family were surprised to see a man driving their wagon and as soon as they saw the state of Rhona's dress they came running to the wagon.

Concern showed on Bill's face as he helped his daughter to the ground. Almost at the same moment Lydia was beside him taking her daughter into her arms and pouring questions at her. Rhona told her story without interruption and Chris saw from the face of the menfolk that it would be a bad day for Blackie should he come face to face with them.

When Rhona had finished her story she was crying again at the recollection of her experience and her mother hurried her away to the other wagon.

'Thanks, young fella, we're mighty grateful for what you did.' Bill held out his hand and Chris felt a warm, firm grip.

'I'm only sorry that she didn't let me accompany her all the way from town, the attack wouldn't have happened then.'

'Shouldn't have sent her on her own, but she's capable and you don't expect this sort of thing to happen. Rhona said you let the man go...'

'Only thing I could do,' cut in Chris not wanting to be too closely questioned on this point. 'I didn't want to leave your daughter and I would have had to do so if I'd had to take the man into town.'

Bill nodded and the conversation drifted away from the attack. Chris knew that he should be going but he did want to see Rhona again. She and her mother appeared a few moments later and Chris saw Rhona, in a new dress, transformed to the girl he had first seen on the wagon in Roundup. He could not take his eyes off her as the two women walked towards them, a situation which Lydia noticed.

'Well, I guess I'd better be going,' said Chris. 'May I call on you again?'

Rhona smiled shyly and glanced at her father.

'Any time. We'd be pleased to see you.' He turned to his sons. 'Kemp bring Chris' horse.'

The youth went to the back of the wagon and unhitched the horse. When he returned he held back from the group who were chatting.

'Come on, boy, come on.' Bill's voice showed irritation at his son's slowness.

The boy held his ground, looked from his father to Chris then back to his father. His face was serious. 'Pa, this horse has a Circle C brand!'

There was a long moment of utter disbelief. The Websters were stunned by Kemp's announcement and Chris cursed deeply to himself for overlooking the simple thing which had betrayed him.

'Circle C!' Bill's gasp came as a long drawn out word. His friendly face had been filled with a hatred which could suddenly explode into violence.

Chris recognised it and realised that he was in a tricky situation which could bring the wrath the Websters felt against the Circle C upon him in the form of physical harm. He did not wait for that to happen. He stepped back, drawing his Colt as he did so.

'I'm sorry to do this,' he said. 'I'm sorry you found out. I can understand your feelings towards the Circle C but believe me I knew nothing about what happened here last night.'

'Come off it son,' rapped Bill.

'It's true,' Chris' words were equally as sharp. 'I knew nothing about it until Rhona told me.' He glanced at the girl. 'The man who attacked you was from the Circle C but he must have done it of his own accord, no one could possibly have known you were going to town, let alone be on your own.'

'If orders hadn't gone out to harass us maybe it wouldn't have entered that man's head to attack Rhona,' stormed Bill. 'Don't try to wriggle away from the blame. If you hadn't that gun in your hand I'd beat the living daylights out of you and send you back as a lesson to the Circle C mob.'

Chris turned to Rhona, a pleading look in his eyes. 'Believe me, please. I do so want to see you again.'

'Get the hell out of here,' thundered Bill, 'before I forget you've got a gun.'

Rhona looked bewildered, a disappointed hurt clouding her face. Tears started to flow and she turned to find comfort from her mother.

'I'll get this matter settled. I'll get the Circle C off your backs,' said Chris.

Bill laughed derisively. 'How do you expect to over-ride the Buck Masters I've heard about?'

'Over-ride him, never. Influence him, maybe. You see I'm his son!'

EIGHT

Seated by the window, Wade Gibson waited impatiently for Johnny's arrival. When he saw him approaching he struggled on to the veranda and, breathing heavily with the exertion, he flopped into a chair. He had taken to this young man last night and he confirmed his feelings as he watched Johnny ride nearer.

'Morning, Mr Gibson,' Johnny greeted with a smile as he stopped his horse.

'Wade, call me Wade, everyone does.'

Johnny swung from his horse and smiled at Wade as he stepped on to the veranda.

'Come and sit down, young fella,' said Wade, a friendly warmth to his voice. 'I knew Kathy would be out looking at the cattle with the foreman this morning, that's why I asked you to come now, I knew we wouldn't be disturbed.'

Johnny was puzzled as to why Wade wanted to see him, a problem which had reoccurred throughout the night but one which he had not been able to solve.

'Kathy told me about you saving Matt and about your theory regarding Red Segal. It's possible. Can't see Buck being behind the trouble. A blusterer, tough, you had to be when he and I came out here. Oh, he's fought to build the Circle C but it's not in his nature to sanction a hanging party, so, as they were Circle C men, it seems to lend credence to your idea about Segal.'

'Glad to know you think the same.' Johnny eyed the older man. 'But you didn't get me here just to confirm what I'd put out as a possibility. You got something in mind?'

Wade's lips parted in a wry smile. 'Yeah.' He paused thoughtfully.

'So, what do we do?' asked Johnny.

'You say we.'

'Sure, that's what I'm here for, isn't it?'

Wade grinned. This young man was quick on the uptake. 'Guess so.'

'Then let's get to the point.'

'I can't get about freely as you know. I have no son. I need someone to act for me. Can't use any of our hands, Kathy might get to know some of the things that it's essential she doesn't know about yet. It came to me last night when we were eating that you could do the job.'

'Thanks for your confidence. I hope I can live up to it.'

'I figure if we can make it look as if Kathy and Chris will come together we might force Segal into acting and showing his hand.'

'You mean tell Kathy and Chris that you want them to act as if they were going to marry?'

'No. It's got to look for real and it might not if we bring them in on the idea, besides too many people in on it and the idea might blow, bring them two in and we'd probably have to bring in Matt and Buck.'

'So, how you figure on doing it?'

'Discredit Matt.'

'What!' Johnny was surprised at this proposition. 'That's playing with people's affections, it's risky.'

'I've thought about that,' replied Wade. 'But I figure if they think a lot about each other they'll come out of it all right.'

'How can you be sure that Segal will act if you throw Kathy and Chris together?'

'I can't, son, I can't. But I figure it this way. If as you say Segal wants to control the Running W and the Circle C through Chris then he ain't going to sit around waiting for me and Buck to die.'

'You figure he'll try and kill you two?'

'Well, maybe not me, I'm not long for this world, but Buck, well he's a different matter. I'd hate to see an old friend fall to the likes of Segal.' He paused for a moment looking hard at Johnny. 'You with me, Johnny?'

'Sure, Wade, sure. I don't like the Segals of this world but I sure hate what we're going to do to Kathy and Chris. What's your plan?'

'Well, Johnny, we'll be branding in a couple of day's time. Matt has permission to brand with his own mark twenty mavericks from among those we take. Strictly that number. Now I reckon…'

By the time Wade had finished explaining his plan Johnny knew that Kathy's father must have spent a great deal of the night going over it again and again to convince himself that it would work. Johnny knew that now it was up to him to implement the idea, he was to be the instrument of Wade's fulfilment. He realised he had a heavy responsibility, that he was going to hurt friends but hoped they would forgive him when the situation had been resolved and the problems which had come to the countryside around Elk River had vanished.

As he rode from the Running W Johnny started to lay his plans very carefully.

'Got me a job, Matt,' said Johnny as he pulled to a halt beside his friend who was brushing down his saddle horse.

Matt's arm stopped in mid-sweep. His smile of greeting vanished and was replaced by a look of disbelief.

'Thought you were staying on to help me,'

he said coolly.

'Sorry, Matt, too good an offer to turn down.'

'That what Mr Gibson wanted you for?'

Johnny nodded.

'Surprised Kathy didn't protest, knowing that you were going to help me.'

'Kathy wasn't there. Wade engaged me. Wanted someone to act for him in things not concerning Kathy and the rest of the outfit seeing that he's more or less confined.'

Matt nodded. 'Suppose it makes sense. Can't expect me to be enthusiastic, it leaves me vulnerable to another hanging party.'

'I figure that won't happen again.'

'Who can tell what lengths Segal will go to.'

Johnny shrugged his shoulders. He stepped on to the veranda. 'I'll get my things.'

Matt did not reply. When he resumed his brushing there was less enthusiasm about it. He hated seeing Johnny go. He'd taken to him, he was grateful to him for saving his life and looked forward to working together and getting to the bottom of the Segal affair.

Now it looked as if that had faded from Johnny's mind.

Johnny came from the house with his few belongings and in a matter of minutes was ready to ride.

'Mr Gibson say anything about branding?' Matt asked.

'Starting in two days time. North section.' Johnny climbed into the saddle. 'I'll be there to give you a hand.' His eyes met Matt's. 'You know, I'll still be around, Matt.' He turned his horse and heeled it into a gallop.

Matt watched him for a few moments wondering if Johnny had meant anything by his final remark.

Blackie, still fuming over Chris's interference, approached the Circle C with some apprehension. Red was going to have to be told and he didn't relish the idea of doing that. He saw Red with two men at one of the corrals which held some unbroken mustangs. He turned his horse in their direction but, when his presence attracted Red's attention, he indicated to the foreman that he would like to see him on his own.

Red climbed from the corral fence and walked towards Blackie who swung from the saddle.

'Well, what you want?' demanded the foreman irritated by Blackie's obvious nervousness.

Blackie wet his lips, trying to pluck up courage to break the news to Red. 'Chris told me to git.' The words were out almost before he realised it.

'What!' Red gasped. He stared incredulously at Blackie. 'When? Why?' Something drastic must have happened; Chris had never taken on this sort of authority before.

Blackie blurted out the whole story before Red could say any more.

'You bloody fool!' lashed Red when Blackie had finished. 'Couldn't you have got a whore in town?'

'I figured you wanted the homesteaders out.'

'Sure, more will follow and they take up

valuable land.'

'Right, so I reckoned this would really have got their craws and they'd have lit out right fast.'

'Maybe they would,' agreed a still annoyed Red. 'Your mistake was in getting caught.'

'How the hell did I know that Chris was around?' Blackie frowned. 'You want me out?'

'Hell, no,' rapped Red.

'If I stick around Chris is going to gun me, but that doesn't bother me, I can outdraw him.'

'Fool, we don't want Chris killed, we want him and Kathy married. You'll have to keep out of sight for a while. If Chris takes a liking to this homesteader girl we're going to be in a mess so we'll just have to get them homesteaders out and eliminate that possibility. I've an idea which Slim and Chuck can work, you keep an eye on Holbrook, we'll deal with him after the homesteaders and there'll be no slipping up this time. Now git before Chris returns.'

139

As he rode to the ranch, Chris tried to calm his anger at the Circle C treatment of the homesteaders. What the hell was his father thinking about? The homesteaders were doing no harm and his father might have known that there were men who would interpret orders for their own ends and Blackie was one of them. Well, he wouldn't be around much longer and woe betide him if he was, after what he had done to Rhona.

Rhona – he could see the look in her eyes when he had revealed he was from the Circle C. He knew she had been hurt but he also saw disappointment and from this he drew the knowledge that she must have liked him. Maybe he could put things right, maybe he could restore the relationship he had sought to develop and which had been approved by the Websters. His anger heightened at the thought of a friendship destroyed.

He was in this frame of mind when he reached the ranch. He did not spare the horse until he was at the house. He slowed it sharply, sprang from the saddle before the animal had stopped and allowed it to run free. He took the steps on to the veranda in two strides and burst into the house.

'Pa!' he yelled as he flung his Stetson on to a chair. 'Pa!' He flung open the door on his right and found his father sitting behind a large mahogany desk. Chris slammed the door behind him and stood glaring at his father.

Buck Masters looked up from the paper he was studying. His face wore a mask of annoyance at the way his son had burst in. 'What the hell's going on?' he demanded.

'That's exactly what I'm asking you,' retorted Chris angrily.

'What you getting at?' snapped Buck, irritated by this banter of words.

'Don't tell me you don't know about the raid on the homesteaders' camp last night.' There was a half sneer to Chris' voice as he challenged his father.

'Don't know what you're talking about,' rapped Buck.

'Come off it, Pa.'

'I don't and that's a fact,' boomed Buck.

Chris met his father's unglinting gaze firmly. 'Pa, I know it happened. Now, come straight, no side tracking, not one way or the other. I want it right down the middle. Did you order any of the men to raid the home-steaders' camp while they were at Gibson's last night?' Chris kept his eyes on his father.

Buck matched look for look, never wavering as he replied. 'I swear I don't know anything about it.' The words were firm and precise, and knowing his father as he did Chris knew he was getting the truth.

'Then what the hell's going on?' said Chris as the anger directed at his father drained away quickly.

Buck watched his son. He was liking what he saw. He knew Chris could be tough in a physical way but he had never seen that toughness directed at other people. Then, he was gentler, apt to give way, something of his mother seemed to predominate. But Buck had suspected there was something of himself deep down, something which needed probing and was only discovered on occasions of extreme provocation. Suddenly Buck felt nearer his son. Chris seemed to sense the feeling and he saw a warmth and respect in his father's eyes.

'Better let me in on it, Chris. What's been happening?' Buck's voice had lost the sharpness of retort.

Chris hesitated a moment then sat down opposite his father and told him the whole story.

'So, knowing your attitude to the homesteaders I figured you'd ordered the raid and then Blackie had used your order for his own ends and attempted to rape Rhona.'

'I ordered no such raid,' said Buck. 'I ranted on to Red after Wade had refused to move the homesteaders on. Maybe Red figured he was complying with my wishes if he gave them a warning.'

'Then tell him to hold off, Pa.'

'You ordering me, son?'

This question suddenly made Chris realise

the attitude he had been taking but he did not regret it and without hesitation replied, 'Sure, Pa. No harassment.'

A broad grin split Buck's face. 'Well I'll be damned.' He pushed himself form his chair and came round the desk to Chris. 'I like it, son, I like it, you giving the orders. Sure, I'll tell Red.'

Buck strode to the door and went out on to the veranda. He saw that Red and the two hands were still with the mustangs. 'Red!' he bellowed. When he saw his foreman look in his direction he added, 'Get in here!' and indicated his desire with a wave of the arm.

'You taken a fancy to this here Rhona?' asked Buck as he re-entered the room.

'Well, I...'

'Never mind,' cut in Buck. 'I can see you have. But what about Kathy and the Running W?'

'Pa, don't let's go into that again.'

'All right,' Buck agreed. 'But just let me say what I've told you before. I don't want to run the two spreads. I just figured a marriage between you two was a logical thing and the biggest spread in Montana would follow.'

Footsteps crossing the wooden veranda terminated any more discussion. Red appeared at the door which Buck had left open.

'You wanted to see me?' Red queried.

'Sure, come on in.'

Red closed the door behind him and moved into the room.

'Did you order the homesteaders' camp to be raided while they were away last night?' asked Buck.

'Well, not exactly. I put Slim and Chuck to keep watch on them figuring that you'd want to know what was happening. Seems they saw the homesteaders leave – looked as if they were heading for the Gibson spread – so Slim and Chuck decided they'd leave them a warning.'

Buck nodded, accepting what seemed a logical explanation.

'Well, call them off. There's to be no more of it!' Red was startled as the words came sharply from Chris.

Red eyed him, his lips tightening into a thin line. He did not like it. Orders from the boss' son! He'd have to teach this upstart his place. Red's piercing glance showed his contempt for Chris.

He looked at Buck. 'You're the boss, Mr Masters, what do you say?'

'Ease off,' replied Buck.

'But they're homesteaders. I thought...'

'Never mind what you thought,' cut in Chris roughly. 'We want them leaving alone.' His emphasis on we left no doubt that he expected he and his father would stay alongside each other on this matter.

Buck nodded his agreement when he saw Red look questioningly at him. 'That's the way it is Red, unless the homesteaders step out of line then we'll think again. But remember, consult us first.' Buck was careful to say us. He liked what he had seen come to the fore in his son and he was going to back it and encourage it.

Red was alarmed by the change in attitudes and this new Chris might prove awkward, but if he hadn't his father to back him... Red's thoughts were left undeveloped as Chris spoke again.

'This morning Blackie tried to rape a homesteader on her way back from town. I told him to collect his things and leave.'

'He's been back. Told me what had happened,' said Red. 'I told him to get on his way.'

Chris nodded. He could tell Red hadn't liked it and wondered if the foreman might react strongly to the new relationship between father and son.

NINE

The Running W was astir early. It was the first day of roundup and branding and meant long, hard days in the open but the men were geared to it and were in a good frame of mind. As arranged, Johnny accompanied them to the north range where he joined Matt to help him pick out, rope and brand the twenty mavericks which Wade was allowing him from among his cattle.

'All set,' Johnny greeted as he turned his horse alongside Matt's.

Matt nodded but said nothing. He was still smarting from what he regarded as Johnny's desertion. His coolness was not lost on Johnny but their relationship was workmanlike throughout the day. They cut out, roped and branded the mavericks efficiently. They made a good team, both

149

knew it but did not comment on it.

The weather held fine and by mid-afternoon on the third day the branding was completed.

As they rose from branding the last maverick Matt's eyes met Johnny's. 'Thanks,' he said.

'That's all right,' replied Johnny. 'You've a find bunch. Good start for you.' He glanced after the young steer now bearing the brand mark which he had just applied. 'Guess I'd better be getting back to see how Wade is.' Still holding the branding iron Johnny started towards his horse.

'You'll only need that iron if you're coming back with me,' said Matt quietly.

Johnny stopped, turned and held out the iron to Matt. 'Sorry,' he said.

Matt took it without a word. He saw Johnny's action as signalling the end of the close relationship which they seemed to have from the moment Johnny had stopped the hanging party. Matt turned and, feeling sick inside, walked to his horse.

Johnny watched him go, cursing the fact that as Matt rode away the branding iron hung from his saddle.

Low thin cloud diffused the moonlight when Johnny slipped from the saddle below the ridge above Matt's house. A short while ago he had seen Matt ride away and from the direction he took he guessed he was going to visit the Websters.

Johnny moved over the ridge and hurried to the wooden building unaware that his presence had startled Blackie Clark who, after checking on the direction of Matt's ride, had just returned to his bedroll, on the opposite side of the river, to settle down for the night. Blackie's curiosity was roused. Who was visiting Holbrook's place after he had gone? And why on foot? Was he afraid a horse might give his presence away? Blackie moved closer to the river to try to make an identification but it was no good, he was too far away and he dared not cross the river and risk discovery.

Johnny came out of the house, hurried up the hill, found his horse and, once mounted, put it into a fast gallop across the grassland to find the cattle on north side of Running W ranch. He urged his animal on, knowing that he must carry out his task with the greatest possible speed. The time of Matt's return was unknown.

Johnny was thankful to find the embers of the Running W branding party still glowing and he quickly fanned them to greater heat. Johnny's face was full of grim determination when he plunged Matt's branding iron into the hot glow. Leaving it to heat up Johnny speedily cut out a Running W steer. He quickly roped it and applied Matt's brand over that of the Running W. Two more steers came under the iron before Johnny left.

He lost no time in riding back to Matt's place but to eliminate the noise of a galloping horse he slowed his animal to a walk as he started up the hill above Elk River. Near the top he slid from the saddle, hurried the remaining distance on foot and from the top of the slope surveyed the house and its surrounding area carefully.

Satisfied that there was no one about, Johnny hurried to the stable. It was with some relief that he found Matt's horse was not there and he lost no time returning the branding iron to the place where he had found it in the house.

He was half way up the hillside when the sound of a horse down by the river sent him to the ground. He flattened himself and stared back in the direction of the noise which had also alerted Blackie.

Clouds unveiled the moon and in the pale light Blackie watched a rider emerge from the trees and ride to the stable. Matt Holbrook had returned. Blackie's relaxation was only momentary, when Matt disappeared inside the stable, for his attention was caught by a movement on the hillside behind the house. A shadowy figure moved quickly up the slope and crossed the ridge.

Blackie was puzzled. Two visitors to Holbrook's house on the same night, both not wanting contact with Holbrook. Or was it the same man making two visits? Blackie concluded that this was more than likely because the visitor on both occasions had come from the same direction. But why? Blackie lay awake for some time but could find no answer to the question.

The following morning Johnny left the house and sought out the Running W foreman.

'Frank, Mr Gibson wants me to ride with you when you look the herd over.'

'Be leaving in ten minutes.' The foreman was friendly but cool. As yet he had not really figured Johnny's role around the Running W. Wade Gibson's righthand man? Well, he wasn't going to stand for any newcomer butting in on his job. Miss Kathy had re-assured him that his foreman's job wasn't in jeopardy, but she had admitted that Johnny's appointment had come as a surprise to her. Sometimes things took an unexpected twist. And this fella was good with cattle. He'd watched him yesterday working with Matt

Holbrook. And he handled a horse well. Now Wade wanted him to look over the cattle. Just what the hell was going on? Frank, straightforward in his thinking, decided to withhold judgement for the time being.

'Branding went well,' observed Johnny, trying to break through Frank's coolness, as they rode at a steady pace towards the north range.

'Yes. I like to look over the bunch we've done before we move 'em. Be doing that this afternoon. Tomorrow we'll be looking for more mavericks.'

'Looks like a good year for the Running W.'

'Should be.'

'Been with Mr Gibson long?'

'Twenty years.'

'Long time.'

'Good boss. Sad about his health. I'll be sorry when he goes.' Frank's words faltered and Johnny knew there was a deep bond of friendship between foreman and boss.

'Guess you've seen some rough times.'

'Sure have. This spread took some building up.'

'Ever have trouble with the Circle C?'

'Good heavens, no.' Frank showed his surprise at the question. 'Wade came out west with Buck Masters. They're the best of friends. Buck will rant and rave and bawl Wade out but there's nothing behind it.'

'Do you figure they could fall out over the homesteaders?'

'No. They're on Running W land with Wade's permission. Buck may rile him about it but he won't go against Wade's authority unless the homesteaders stepped out of line but even then it would be a joint move.'

Johnny was pleased to have the opinion of a man who had known both ranch owners for so long.

'Would the same apply in the case of Holbrook?'

'Sure.'

'Has Red Segal been with Masters long?'

'Three years. Can't say I've taken to him. Don't like his cronies. But he's a good foreman and knows his job.'

They reached the cattle quietly grazing under the warm Montana sun, and the two men cast expert eyes over the herd, but Johnny's sought one thing in particular. Time moved on. Johnny grew uneasy. Frank would soon be calling time. He must find what he was looking for before then. He grew tense. His eyes probed swiftly. He moved with more urgency. Then he saw it and relief swept over him as he halted his horse.

'Hi, Frank, get over here,' he shouted.

The urgent note brought Frank turning his horse sharply and tapping it into a trot towards Johnny.

'Look, there,' said Johnny, indicating the brand mark on the nearest steer.

'What the hell? That brand's been changed.' Frank edged his horse nearer the steer. His eyes narrowed. 'Holbrook!' He glanced sharply at Johnny. 'You worked with him when we were branding.'

'Only mavericks,' replied Johnny answering Frank's unspoken question.

'The fool must have come back and done this,' commented the foreman. 'How the hell did he expect to get away with it?'

'He probably didn't know you came back to inspect the herd. Matt likely expected to be able to cut that steer out, with the ones that are rightfully his, without you noticing.'

'Fool, after the way Wade and Kathy have treated him. They'll move him on, and Kathy ain't going to like that, she and Holbrook have been seeing a lot of each other lately. C'm on, let's see if there are any more.'

Their search revealed two more then Frank decided to return to the ranch.

'Can't understand it.' Frank shook his head sadly. 'Likeable young fella too.'

Once clear of the cattle the two men put their horses into a gallop for the Running W.

The urgency of their approach captured the attention of Kathy and her father who were talking over ranching policy on the veranda of their house.

'Something's wrong, Pa,' said Kathy as she got to her feet to view the two horsemen.

She frowned. Frank and Johnny had gone to look over the cattle on the north range and a return ride as swift as this could mean they'd found trouble there.

The two men pulled their horses to a halt and were quickly out of the saddles to reply to the unspoken query on Kathy's face.

'Found some cattle overbranded,' gasped Frank as he drew air deep into his lungs.

'Overbranded?' Wade appeared puzzled.

'Yes,' replied Frank. He glanced at Kathy. 'I'm sorry to say this, Kathy, the overbrand is Matt Holbrook's.'

'What!' Kathy stared in wide-eyed amazement at this news. 'There must be some mistake.' She looked sharply at Johnny hoping he would contradict Frank's statement.

'It's Holbrook's brand all right,' Johnny confirmed.

'But I ... I don't understand. Why should he want to do it? We let him have twenty mavericks.'

'Seems he wants more.'

'But why leave the cattle after putting his

brand on them? If he'd done it he'd take the cattle, not leave them to be found.'

'He wouldn't expect an inspection,' Johnny pointed out. 'And it would be an easy matter for him to take these along with the others.'

Disbelief which still ruled her heart showed in Kathy's eyes. This couldn't be true, she didn't want it to be true. Not Matt. She turned to her father hoping he wasn't going to order action which every cattleman would take if his trust had been broken.

Wade met the pleading look in his daughter's eyes but he looked beyond her at Frank and Johnny. 'Move him on!' The order was curt, sharp, precise and indicated to his men that he expected no-nonsense action from them.

'No!' Kathy's cry halted Frank and Johnny as they turned away. 'Pa give Matt a chance to explain.'

'What is there to explain? The evidence must be there. He can't talk against that.' Wade nodded to the two men indicating that he wanted his order carrying out.

They went down the steps to their horses. Kathy looked desperately at her father.

'Pa, please, you've got to stop them.'

'No, Kathy. Matt's betrayed our trust. I know you were sweet on him and if he'd thought anything about you he wouldn't have done this.' Wade felt for his daughter and was sorry for the pain he was causing her. 'It's a good job he was found out before it was too late. He's got to go.'

Tears welled in Kathy's eyes. She looked round anxiously as Frank and Johnny sent their horses away. 'I'm going too, Pa! There must be some explanation.'

She was off the steps and running to the stable ignoring her father's shout of 'Kathy! No! Come back!'

Stifling her tears she called for the stable-man who saddled her horse quickly, urged on by the impatient Kathy who feared that Matt would resist the two men.

As soon as the horse was ready she was into the saddle and urging it across the grassland towards Elk River.

Kathy's thoughts, anxious for Matt's safety, were thrown into confusion by the change in Johnny. From being a friend to Matt he was now riding to hound him off the land and out of the region around the Running W. Why had he altered? Had he seen some hidden streak in Matt which she had not discovered? Her thoughts whirled and then her mind was pounded into one urgency by the thrum of the beating hooves, she must get to Matt first.

Matt Holbrook was by the river when the tattoo of hard-ridden horses brought him straightening and turning in alarm. His experience at the hands of the Circle C had alerted him to hear trouble in such a sound. But these horses were crossing Running W land, nevertheless the riders need not be from the Running W. Matt waited no longer. He raced for the house and emerged with his rifle just as two men came over the rise and sent their horses towards the building.

Johnny and Frank! Relief swept over Matt. Tension flowed from his body and he relaxed. He wondered about the urgency of their ride but he saw no danger in it. He laid his rifle down against the veranda rails and, leaning on them, watched the two riders approach.

As they fronted the veranda, Frank and Johnny split, widening the distance between them so that it was more difficult for Matt to keep a close watch on them both at the same time. This action puzzled Matt and, coupled with the serious expression on their faces, brought a tinge of alarm to his mind. He automatically tensed, as if these men were enemies, and he wished he hadn't laid his rifle down. But these riders were friends so what the...? He glanced sharply from one to the other but could glean nothing about the nature of their visit from their expressions.

'Holbrook, we want you out of here right now!' Frank's tone was biting, commanding, requiring instant obedience without question.

Matt was so taken aback by this order that

he just stared dumbly at the speaker.

'Off this land, so move!' Frank's words bit more fiercely and their impact brought home their full meaning.

'What the hell?' Matt's eyes turned from Frank to Johnny hoping for contradiction but all he found was confirmation in the cold muzzle of Johnny's Colt. He stared in disbelief. 'Johnny, what's going on?'

'Like Frank says, you gotta leave.' Johnny's voice was cold.

'Leave? Why?' The words were almost challenging as Matt tore his gaze back to Frank.

'Holbrook, Mr Gibson gave you permission to brand twenty mavericks. That was generous. There was no cause to return and alter the brand on some Running W cattle. That smells of rustling.'

Matt stared for a moment, hardly able to believe his ears, then he suddenly exploded. 'Rustling! What the hell are you talking about?' His eyes blazed angrily.

'We examined the cattle on the north range

earlier this morning and found three Running W steers overbranded with your mark.'

'Johnny and I branded twenty mavericks and no more,' rapped Matt. 'That so, Johnny?'

'Sure,' Johnny agreed.

'Right,' snapped Frank, 'you should have left it at that. Why return and brand some more?'

'I didn't.'

'You seen 'em, Johnny?' Frank called across to him, seeking support for his statements.

'I saw them.'

Matt was flabbergasted. These two men wouldn't make it up. They had no cause to. They wouldn't come accusing unless they had evidence. But how had it happened?

'I didn't do it. Someone must have stolen my branding iron.'

Ignoring the two men who faced him, Matt spun round and disappeared into the house. The two horsemen were not going to be caught out, they were not going to let him pull another gun. They dropped from their

165

saddles and followed him into the house. Matt went to a high shelf and felt on it, then slowly he lifted down his branding iron. He stared at it in disbelief. It shouldn't be there, yet it was. Still gazing at it he turned round slowly and then lifted his eyes to the two men who covered him with their Colts.

'Stolen?' Frank's question was mocking and contained the significance that he would stand no more questioning, no more resistance.

Matt read it in Frank's face. He was shattered. He shrugged his shoulders. He was mystified. He couldn't begin to understand what was happening to him. He felt numb. He let the iron fall from his limp fingers to the floor. What else could he do but go? Resignedly he started to gather up a few belongings.

The sound of a galloping horse brought him straightening, wondering, his mind grasping at the slightest possibility which would end this nightmare. Someone coming to refute these accusations? He glanced at

Johnny and Frank and saw from their expressions that he was wrong. They had both guessed that the rider was Kathy and they were not surprised when she burst into the room.

'Matt!' Kathy cried, her eyes wide with anxiety. She stared at the belongings he was packing into his saddle-bags. 'You aren't...? You didn't...?' The fact that Matt was making to leave hit Kathy hard. Why pack up if you were not guilty? Why give up without a protest if you'd done no wrong?

The train of Kathy's thoughts must have shown in her face for Matt gave her one long look and said with quiet accusation, 'You too, Kathy?'

'No, Matt, no!' she started but her voice trailed away when her eyes rested on the branding iron on the floor. She stared at it for a moment then looked up at Frank, a man she had known and trusted ever since she was a little girl.

He saw her questioning look, saw the hurting ache in her heart but he knew it was better if he held nothing back. 'Sorry, Kathy,' he said quietly. 'I've seen the cattle. Johnny's seen the cattle and that's the iron which changed the brand.' There was a finality about his words.

Tears welled in Kathy's eyes. 'Why, Matt, why?' Her words were a mixture of accusation and a pleading for an explanation.

Matt ignored her and went on packing. What was the use of trying to explain when he didn't know the answer? What was the use of protesting. The evidence was stacked against him. Who had framed him and why? Better to go quietly now and hope to stick around long enough to find the answers to the riddles which raised more than puzzling thoughts in his mind.

He fastened the bags, straightened, glanced round the room and said quietly, 'Guess that'll do.' He ignored Kathy and the two men as he walked from the house. They followed, Frank with a comforting arm round Kathy's shoulders. Matt picked up his rifle under Johnny's close scrutiny, stepped from the veranda, climbed on his horse and, without a word or glance at the three people who, not so long ago, had been his friends, rode to the top of the rise and turned his horse to follow the Elk River upstream.

TEN

Kathy was out of the saddle quickly and, with tears streaming down her face, she rushed on to the veranda and fell on to her knees beside her father's chair. She buried her head against his shoulder and he put his arm round her with loving tenderness and gently stroked her hair. He hated having to use his own daughter to flush Red Segal out and he hoped she would understand when explanations were made.

'He's on his way, boss.' Frank's words were quiet as if he didn't want to interrupt this moment between father and daughter.

Wade nodded. Frank and Johnny turned their horses in the direction of the bunkhouse.

'Want to see you shortly, Johnny,' Wade called.

Johnny raised his hand in acknowledgement and rode on.

Wade let Kathy cry some then gently raised her head. 'I'm sorry, Kathy. I didn't want you to go.'

Kathy wiped her eyes and forced her tears to stop. 'I had to, Pa. I had to know about Matt. Pa, he left without a protest.' Kathy's bewildered expression tore at Wade. He wanted to ease her pain, wanted to tell her the truth but he dare not. One split in his plan to flush out Red Segal and the whole thing might foul up. 'Why did he do it, Pa? He didn't have to.'

'I don't know, Kathy. Maybe it's in him, maybe it's his make-up. Better for you to know now.'

'Guess so.' She looked hard at her father through her damp eyes. 'It might have been best if Chris and I...' Her voice faltered.

'Don't worry about that now, but maybe you're right. Chris and you married might solve a lot of things. You and he think a lot about each other, I think you'd have married him if Matt hadn't come along. A pity he did.'

Kathy leaned forward and kissed her father. 'I'm sorry for all the fuss I've caused. You'll like to see me settled before you...' Kathy's voice trailed away.

Wade smiled wanly. 'Before I die? Of course I would but I don't want to rush you. You're sensible, I know you'll do the right thing even if I'm not here to see it.'

Kathy flung her arms around his neck and they held each other for a few minutes.

From the bench outside the bunk-house, Johnny saw Kathy leave her father and he came over to the house to give Wade a full report of what had happened.

'Fine,' said the Running W owner when Johnny had finished his story. 'That gets Matt out of the way and when Red Segal hears about it I hope he plays it the way I expect. Johnny, I want you to keep an eye on Buck, I'd hate anything to happen to him because of what I might have set in motion.'

'I'll take care of things,' replied Johnny

with a reassurance that comforted Wade.

Puzzled by the sight of Running W guns turned on Matt Holbrook, Blackie watched the young man ride away from his home. After Kathy and the two men had left, Blackie followed Matt, easily holding him in sight, for Matt kept to the heights above the river.

Blackie watched him arrive at the homesteaders' encampment and, once he felt sure that Matt was staying, he decided that the events he had witnessed had better be relayed to Red Segal as soon as possible.

Heeding the threat which hung over him from Chris, Blackie took the utmost caution to approach the Circle C. He left his horse hidden by the rise behind the buildings and using every available cover made for the stables. He passed through them cautiously, surveyed the back of the house and the space between the stables and the bunkhouse. All was still. He chose the moment to move and then ran swiftly across the intervening ground. He slipped into the bunkhouse quietly and was thankful that his supposition, that it would be empty at this time of day, was correct. Six strides took him to the door which led to Red's quarters. He tapped lightly on it and was surprised to hear a call of 'Come in.'

'Blackie! You're running a risk coming here. I thought we'd arranged...' There was a touch of annoyance to Red's astonishment.

'I figured it was important enough,' cut in Blackie. 'I'm surprised but glad to find you here. I was prepared to wait until you showed up.'

Red nodded, waited for Blackie to continue and listened to his story without interrupting.

'You figure Holbrook's gone for good, run out by the Running W?' said Red when Blackie had finished.

'Looked mighty like it to me. Frank Sommers and this here new fella Johnny Clinton both had guns on him and kept it that way until Holbrook rode off. I was puzzled when I saw Clinton, thought he was friendly with Holbrook.'

'Heard a rumour in town that he'd gone working for the Running W.'

'The homesteaders appeared to welcome Holbrook but, I guess if he stays there, Webster will be concerned in case the Running W find he's hanging around with them.'

Red smiled. 'Looks as though the Running W's done our job for us and got rid of Holbrook. Wonder why? But that doesn't matter to us.' Red looked thoughtful. 'That looks like the end of romance between Kathy and Holbrook. Maybe she'll turn to Chris, so, as we planned, we get the homesteaders out of the way so Chris doesn't get ideas about the homesteader girl and we take care of Buck. We'll move tonight. You get back and keep an eye on the homesteaders from the usual place on our side of the river so Slim and Chuck will know where to contact you.'

Blackie left the Circle C using the same

precautions as when he arrived and rode quickly to take up his watch on the bank of Elk River.

Darkness was creeping across the prairie when Slim and Chuck singled out the steer they wanted. Cutting it off from the rest of the cattle they drove it until they reached Elk River some distance upstream from the homesteaders' camp. By the moonlight, filtering through the trees, they quickly slaughtered the animal, and removed a hind quarter which they cut up into smaller, more manageable pieces.

Carrying two pieces of meat each, they made their way quietly along the river bank, crossed to the opposite side at a suitable place and approached the homesteaders' camp. From an advantageous position they studied it for some time, until they were satisfied that the camp had settled for the night.

Slim tapped Chuck on the shoulder, the pre-arranged signal for him to slip away quietly and use the Indian in him to approach the nearest wagon without raising the alarm. He lifted the canvas flap at the back of the wagon and peered inside. By the dim light from the moon he saw that what he sought was not there. A few seconds later scrutiny of the second wagon revealed what he wanted – the store wagon.

He dropped to the ground and made a quick survey of the camp. No one moved. He glanced skywards and a few moments later when clouds dimmed the moon he snaked across the open ground to the trees and joined Slim.

'Second wagon,' he whispered.

Slim nodded. Without another word they gathered their meat and edged as near to the second wagon as they could before breaking cover. With a wary eye cast in the direction of the sleeping forms they reached the wagon and deposited the meat inside. As they turned to go someone stirred in their bedding. Slim and Chuck froze, their hands resting on the butts of their Colts. They waited, tense, ready to draw. The movement stopped and stillness settled over the camp once again. The two men relaxed and quickly made their way to the cover of the trees.

Reaching their horses they rode away from the river, circled and came to the pre-arranged meeting place with Blackie.

All three were awake by first light and by the time the homesteaders were stirring to a new day Slim, Chuck and Blackie had their concentrated attention directed at the camp.

The eastern horizon was brightening with a new day when Red Segal watched the Circle C cowboys ride away to continue the branding. Twenty minutes later he was in the stable and had just started to saddle his horse when he heard footsteps approaching the stable. He glared in the direction of the door and saw Chris come in.

'Riding far?' asked Red casually when Chris threw a saddle on his horse.

'Town,' replied Chris. 'Want to see the bank manager and I'll call on the blacksmith and arrange for him to come out and shoe those horses we broke last week.'

'Good,' replied Red. 'That'll save me.'

Both men went about their tasks without another word, Red making sure that he took longer than Chris for he did not want him to know that he was going to saddle a second horse.

When Chris had his mount ready he led it from the stable, mounted and left the Circle C. Red watched him go and, satisfied that Chris was riding in the direction of town, he returned to prepare the second animal.

Johnny blinked and opened his eyes to a light which was beginning to creep across the sky. He stretched and eased the stiffness form his body. Suddenly he was intensely awake. A jumble of noises drifted up the hill behind the Circle C buildings to the ridge on which he had prepared to keep watch on Buck Masters. He threw his blanket aside and, twisting on to his stomach, crawled to the top of the rise.

He watched the early morning movements

at the ranch as the Circle C men prepared to leave. Calculating their numbers as they left he was aware that only three men remained on the property and a short while later, when he saw Chris leave, he was alarmed to realise that left Buck and Red alone at the ranch.

Johnny moved swiftly, with caution, towards the single door at the rear of the stable. His eyes alert, probed everywhere ready to signal instant action should any-thing indicate that he had been seen. He was relieved when he reached the wooden building without discovery. He edged his way to the open door, paused and listened.

Someone was in there! Johnny peered round the door-post with care. A man, with his back to him was saddling a horse. As he turned to leave the stall Johnny saw he was Red Segal.

When the Circle C foreman left the stable by the wide doors at the front, Johnny stepped inside, ran quickly to the doorway and was just in time to see Red going into the bunk-house. Johnny decided to use the loft as his look-out point and hurried to the ladder. He was just about to climb up when he realised that something had made an impression on his mind but he was not immediately certain what it was. He turned round from the ladder. Puzzled he looked around for the thing which had caught his subconscious. His eyes moved around to the saddled horse and then beyond it to the next stall. An excitement gripped him. That was it! A second horse was saddled! Only Red had been in the stable. Had he saddled them both? If so why? Only he and Buck were on the ranch. Were they going to take a ride together? Was this part of Red's plan?

With his thoughts tumbling over the possibilities Johnny climbed the ladder to the loft. He couldn't have had a better vantage point. He checked his Colt and waited.

ELEVEN

Lydia Webster stirred under her horse-hide blanket. She blinked her eyes open. It was daylight but, judging by the feel of the morning and the low sun it was early. Her husband still slept under his blanket beside her. Gently, so as not to disturb him, she raised herself on one elbow and looked around the encampment. No one else was awake. She sank down again and lay gazing at the clear sky.

It was going to be another warm day and no doubt another night to sleep in the open. She wished they had a roof over their heads, a house, a place of permanence. She was tired of being pushed on, never finding anywhere where they could feel safe. She had hoped this would be the place, beside the Elk River, especially after the friendly reception they had received from the Gibson's, but after the raid on the deserted camp and the attack on Rhona she wondered if they would ever find peace where all cattlemen were friendly.

She'd had high hopes of Wade Gibson's influence but even those had gone with the arrival of Matt Holbrook, and his story of being turned off his place by the Running W. She realised the Running W would turn against them if Matt was found here, but he had pleaded innocence and she and Bill had agreed that they could not turn him away until they knew more of the truth. Lydia sighed and wondered what life would bring.

A quarter of an hour later Bill stirred. He turned over, saw his wife was awake, shuffled nearer and kissed her. She returned his kiss, feeling a comfort and safety in his nearness.

'Guess we ought to be up,' he whispered. 'There's a lot to do.'

She smiled, nodded and kissed him again.

Bill woke the rest of the sleepers and,

while they prepared for a new day, he stirred the fire embers into a bright heat.

Lydia breathed deeply of the clean air as she walked to the store-wagon to get some things for breakfast. She turned back the canvas covering the rear of the wagon and fastened it, then lowered the tail-board. She reached for the things she wanted but as her hand closed on them she froze and stared in amazement at the four lumps of meat which lay in the wagon.

Her mind went numb for a few seconds and then became a whirl of alarming thoughts. Meat they ought not to have! Surely Bill hadn't risked their chances of settlement. But if he hadn't, who had? How had it got there? Lydia pulled herself up sharply. This was no way to be going on. There was only one thing to do.

'Bill!' she called. 'Get over here.'

Bill looked up from the fire. He detected a note of concern in Lydia's voice. It may not be noticeable to the others but he hadn't been married to her for nigh on twenty-five years without knowing her reaction when something troubled her. He dropped the stick which he was holding and went to her.

'Something wrong?' he asked.

She did not speak but indicated the inside of the wagon.

Bill looked in and a long gasp of surprise broke from his lips. 'Where's that come from?'

'I don't know. I thought you might tell me.'

'No idea,' replied Bill. His lips tightened. He reached into the wagon and picked up a lump of meat. 'Not long killed.'

'Bill, if we're caught with meat we shouldn't have...' She left the frightening consequences unspoken.

'I know,' said Bill grimly. 'Matt?'

'Surely he wouldn't, but who else?'

'And where's the rest of the carcass? If it's still lying around where it can be found...' He left the sentence unfinished and reached for another lump of meat. 'I'm going to get rid of it. Clean up any evidence when I've gone. We'll say nothing about it.' He turned from the wagon but froze in his movement. 'Damn!'

Three horsemen were crossing the ford!

He swung round and threw the meat back in the wagon. 'Cover them,' he said sharply.

Anxiety gnawed at Lydia's stomach as she did his bidding. She felt sick. In a numbed daze she unfastened the canvas and let it fall over the back of the wagon.

'Occupy yourself Lydia, act as if nothing had happened.'

The horsemen were out of the river and coming in quickly towards the camp. Lydia hurried to busy herself with the fire. Kemp and Ed stopped what they were doing and stood watching the riders. Rhona's eyes took in the horsemen with her first glance. A chill swept through her and fear gripped her heart. For a moment she could not move then panic filled inside her and sent her legs seeking protection. She ran to her father who, seeing the fright in her eyes, held out his left arm and enfolded her with it as she pressed herself close to him, sensing in his nearness and touch the safety she desired.

'Pa, the one on the left, he's the one who nearly…' Her voice faltered and faded away, leaving the horror of the unspoken words pounding in her father's mind.

Bill's eyes narrowed as he concentrated on the dark rider. Circle C!

Blackie grinned when he saw the girl's reaction.

Bill, still with his arm round Rhona, stood his ground as the three riders pulled to a halt in front of him.

'Just found a carcass of a Circle C steer. Some meat gone. Know anything about it?' Slim's voice was sharp with anger.

Bill's mind raced. Was there any use denying that there was meat in the wagon? Wouldn't these men hold them at gun point and make a search? If he told them what he knew they might just believe him, and if Holbrook had put the meat in the wagon it would give him a chance to admit it and exonerate the Websters.

'All I know is that there's meat in that wagon, four lumps, but I don't know how it got there.'

Lydia straightened from the fire. She couldn't believe what she was hearing. Bill had told her to cover the meat up and now he was admitting it was there. What was he thinking about?

Slim gave a harsh laugh and glanced at his two companions. 'Doesn't know how it got there,' he said derisively.

'I don't!' snapped Bill. 'My wife found it when she went to get some things for breakfast.'

Slim's eyes narrowed as he leaned forward on his saddle-horn and pierced Bill with his gaze. 'I'll tell you how it got there. You killed a Circle C steer. Hid it among the trees upstream, cut some off and brought it back here. Simple isn't it?'

Bill stiffened. He met Slim's intense gaze. 'I know nothing about it,' he said firmly.

Slim ignored him. 'Take a look, Blackie,'

he said.

Blackie rode over to the wagon, lifted the flaps and peered inside. He swung out of the saddle on to the tail-board and went into the wagon. A few moments later he looked out and shouted, 'It's here, covered up.'

'Covered up!' Slim grinned at Bill. 'Seems to me you were trying to hide it.'

Bill's mind was awhirl. He'd forgotten he'd told Lydia to cover it up. Fool. This made it look as if he had known it was there and tried to hide it. He was trapped. He glanced at Matt hoping for an explanation but he saw from the expression on Matt's face that he was puzzled by the whole affair. They were finished. They'd have to move. The meat must have been planted for just this reason. Circle C again.

For a moment Bill was tempted to defy and challenge the Circle C riders with this idea, but they must have sensed his belligerence for they slid their Colts from their holsters and Bill saw his family facing an argument he was powerless to combat.

Once clear of the Circle C and the prying eyes of Red Segal, Chris turned his horse off the trail and headed for Elk River and the homesteaders' encampment. He felt he had allowed enough time to pass to bring some calmness to the situation and that now he should set things straight and let them know that his father had nothing to do with what had happened, that it was all the result of an over zealous foreman taking his father's remarks too far, and that from now on there would be no harassment.

Chris kept to a brisk pace and topped the rise opposite the ford expecting to see the homesteaders going about their normal morning chores. Instead, the sight of three men threatening the Websters with drawn guns sent him wheeling his horse below the ridge. He dropped from the saddle and ran quickly to the top of the rise over which he peered to take in the scene in more detail.

Slim! Chuck! Blackie! The names thundered in his mind but Blackie's banged loudest. He'd warned Blackie, yet he was still around and with Circle C men who must have been warned not to harass the homesteaders.

Chris turned and ran back to his horse. He climbed into the saddle and turned the animal upstream, coming down to the river only when he knew he was out of sight of the encampment. He urged the horse across the water and once on the other side rode downstream for a hundred yards before leaving the animal securely fastened to a tree.

Chris moved quickly but silently towards the camp. The scene was one of feverish activity as the homesteaders prepared to leave and escape from the laughing, cajoling Circle C men who mocked and insulted the homesteaders. On more than one occasion both Bill and Matt were stung to retaliate against the ribald remarks directed at Rhona, but they kept a tight check on their instincts, knowing that their three harassers would not hesitate to use the guns which hovered menacingly all the time.

Chris weighed the situation up carefully. He had to get close. To attempt anything from too far would only endanger the Websters. Chris knew he had to offer his physical presence at a range which would occupy the three men's full attention and hope he could get them before they got him.

He moved carefully until he was opposite the nearest wagon, then, judging the right moment, he hurried across the intervening space covered from the people in the camp by the wagon. He paused a moment and peered cautiously round the end of the wagon. The three Circle C men were in a close group with their backs to him as they watched Rhona.

Chris stepped round the end of the wagon and walked towards them.

'Blackie!' This one word had the effect of freezing the whole camp into temporary immobility. Homesteaders' eyes turned to him, finding a new hope in the call. The three Circle C men, incredulous that anyone should interfere, turned slowly.

'Thought I gave you the sack, Blackie. Why are you still riding with Circle C men?' Chris watched the three men intensely, concentrating, watching for the slightest hostile move. 'I told you what would happen if I met you again.' The words were cold, threatening.

Blackie licked his lips. He didn't like the situation but he forced a grin to give the impression of confidence, after all hadn't he two guns to back him?

Chris' eyes narrowed almost imperceptibly, drawing the men, particularly Blackie, into sharper focus. His gaze never wavered from Blackie's eyes although he took all three in at once. He saw Blackie's eyes harden with a coldness. This was the moment. Chris' right hand moved. Blackie's gun was coming up. The Colt on Chris' thigh cleared its leather. In a continuation of the flowing movement the gun was on its target, a finger squeezed the trigger an instant before Blackie's closed round his.

In that instant Chris flung himself sideways. He hit the ground and rolled over. A second shot took Slim in the thigh but Slim's bullet clipped Chris' arm while Chuck's whined unpleasantly close to his head. Slim crashed to the ground beside Blackie, whose shirt was spreading the blood oozing from his side.

Chris saw Chuck's gun swinging on him again. There was a loud roar and Chuck lurched forward, his eyes widening with the acceptance of the unexpected. His Colt roared but its aim had been displaced. He staggered and pitched to the ground to lie still, face down in the dust. Chris looked beyond Chuck to see who had pulled him back from the edge of death. He saw a grim-faced Matt with his Colt in his hand. As he scrambled to his feet Chris saw that Bill had acted with equal swiftness and stood threatening the two wounded men.

Chris nodded to Matt. 'Thanks,' he said, then turned his attention to the two men on the ground. 'I want answers and I want them quick.' His voice was harsh indicating that he wanted the truth and would stand no nonsense and stop at nothing to get it. 'Segal was told to stop harassing the home-steaders so what goes on?'

Both men looked sullen. Blackie winced with pain which brought a tightness to his lips and drained his face of colour leaving the scar on his cheek standing out vividly. His eyes bore into Chris with a deep-set hatred. 'To hell with you!' he spat. The effort to speak sent pain coursing through his body. He jerked under its impact. His whole body tightened and he drew hard on his breath. His eyes widened. Then sud-denly his body went limp and he lay still.

Chris was unmoved by the death. He felt little remorse at killing this man. He turned to Slim. 'Well?' he demanded.

'We found a dead Circle C steer. Meat had been cut from it, that meat is in Webster's wagon!'

Chris was staggered by this statement. If this was true then he had been wrong to move as he had except against Blackie, for that he had some justification. Chris kept a tight hold on his thoughts which threatened to run away with him. He had to keep cool and think clearly.

'If that's true you shouldn't have taken steps against the homesteaders without authority.' He gave Slim no chance to reply but turned to Bill. 'Is this true?'

Bill met Chris' gaze firmly. He saw the young man's eyes probing to see if he got the truth. 'There's meat in the wagon. Lydia discovered it when she went to get some things for breakfast. I don't know how it got there, I didn't put it there and that's the honest truth. If Matt didn't then I figure it could be a frame-up by the Circle C.'

'Hold it,' rapped Chris. 'Not the Circle C. My father knew nothing about the raid on your camp and as I've just said when he heard about it he ordered no more harassment.' He glanced at Matt. 'Know anything about that meat?'

'No. There's something queer going on. The Websters have been wrongly accused

197

and were about to be driven off until you came along, and I've been kicked off my place, wrongly accused by the Running W of overbranding some of their cattle.'

'I don't know about your *trouble* but I sure mean to find out about this.' Chris turned and looked hard at Slim. 'Well, what do you have to say?'

'I've told you, the evidence is in the wagon.'

'Put there by someone else,' snapped Bill towering over the wounded man. 'Most likely you.'

'Matt, see if there are any knives in their saddlebags,' said Chris.

Matt nodded and went to the horses. Chris kept his eyes on Slim and he saw him cast a furtive look after Matt. Apprehension crossed his face and he licked his dried lips knowing what Matt would find. He glanced back at Chris and was startled to see the young man's eyes on him and he realised that Chris had read his fears.

'Well, going to talk?' Chris' cold stare sent

a chill through Slim.

Slim recognised the hopelessness of the situation and this set his mind on saving his own hide.

'Give me a break?' he asked. 'I'll talk if you'll let me ride out of here without any strings.'

Chris looked thoughtful for a moment. 'Right, but miss nothing out or it'll be the worse for you.'

Slim's hesitation was only fractional while he gathered his thoughts and then he started on the story of Red Segal's plans to control and run the Circle C and Running W and to milk off profits for his own advantage.

Everyone was astonished but none more so than Chris who listened in amazement as Slim revealed a situation about which he and his father had been totally unaware. Chris' hatred of Segal mounted as the story was told so that, by the time Slim had come to the end, Chris had one desire, to seek out and eliminate Segal before he could do any more harm.

'Where's Segal now?' Chris demanded as he fought to keep control of his seething anger.

'At the ranch. He's making sure your Pa stays there so that, once we return and give him the word that the homesteaders have been moved on, your father can be taken for a ride from which he would not return, but his end would look like an accident.'

Although alarm for his father's safety seized him Chris drew some consolation from the fact that Red was not going to make a move until he heard from his side-kicks. Nevertheless he sensed danger for his father unless things were handled carefully.

Chris glanced at Bill. 'Sorry to leave you with this, but keep Slim here until you hear from me. If my Pa's all right then he can go, if not...' Chris left Slim to think on the threat.

'Sure,' said Bill, accepting the responsibility.

Without a word to anyone else Chris

hurried to find his horse beside Elk River and when he returned to cross the ford he found Matt already in the saddle waiting for him.

They put their horses across the river and once on the other side sent them into a fast gallop to the Circle C.

TWELVE

Red Segal, keeping watch from the bunk-house, stiffened into alertness when he saw the broad frame of Buck Masters appear at the back door of the house. He cursed when Buck started towards the stables. This was not what he wanted. Now he would have to show his hand to Buck before the others returned from driving off the homesteaders. It could be tricky especially if anyone else showed. But Red knew he had no choice but to detain Buck. He drew his Colt, checked it with a quick glance and watched Buck go to the stable.

From the loft in the stable, Johnny watched Buck Masters come from the house and walk briskly to the stable. His alertness was relaxed. He was thankful something was happening. Maybe this would force Red into doing something and whatever it was Johnny was ready for it.

Buck reached the stable and went inside. Johnny flattened himself and, from the high loading door in the loft, peered cautiously outside in the direction of the bunk-house. As he had expected the door opened and Red Segal stepped outside. Much to Johnny's relief he saw the Circle C foreman slipping his Colt back into its leather. At least there wasn't going to be a killing in cold blood. Johnny slid silently across the loft until he could see down into the stable.

Buck went to the stall in which his horse was kept and was startled to find it saddled. He was puzzling over this strange situation when he heard someone come into the stable and turned to see who it was.

'Red, know who saddled my horse?' Buck asked.

'Me, about half an hour ago.'

Red's statement startled Buck. 'You? Why?'

'I knew you'd want it.'

'But you couldn't. I've only just decided

I'd ride over to see Wade.'

Red smiled and his eyes mocked with the look of a man presuming himself to be in an unassailable position. 'Sure I did. You and I are taking a ride as soon as Slim, Chuck and Blackie get back.'

'What the hell are you talking about?' Buck showed his annoyance at statements which bore no meaning to him. 'Besides Blackie was given the sack.'

'I signed him on again straight away.'

'What!' Buck was amazed at his foreman's defiance. 'You were told to...'

'You don't tell me any more.' There was a smirk on Red's face as he let the words come smoothly but with a definition which left no doubt in Buck's mind that what he said was true.

Buck's eyes narrowed and his face darkened with an anger which was swelling inside him in contest with Red's defiance. 'What goes on, Segal?' he demanded.

In the loft Johnny was tense. Could things move to an explosive head here in the stable? His hand closed round the butt of his Colt but he was in no position to get off a carefully aimed shot at Segal who was almost hidden by the side of the stall. But Johnny's mind eased when he recalled that Red had stated that he was waiting for his three sidekicks and then they would take a ride. Red wouldn't want a killing here on the ranch, it had to occur elsewhere and probably made to look like an accident.

He had his assumptions confirmed when Red answered Buck's question. 'Just that I'm taking over. To do that I need you out of the way. That ride we're going to take, an accident will occur. When Chris marries Kathy and needs me to run the joint Circle C and Running W – well you can see the situation.' Red grinned at the look of amazement on Buck's face but the sharpness of his concentration did not waver and, when he saw Buck's move for his Colt, Red cleared leather faster and Buck's draw faltered.

'Leave it!' rapped Red viciously.

'You bastard. You'll never get away with it.'

Frustration showed in Buck's voice as he let his gun slip back into its leather holster.

'Of course I will,' grinned Red. 'Who'll stop me?'

'Even if you get rid of me you'll still have Chris to contend with.'

Red laughed loudly. 'That weak-kneed...' There was derision in the voice which Buck interrupted harshly.

'You've underestimated Chris,' he fumed. 'You're in for a big surprise if you think you can control him. He's changed or rather the tough side of Chris is just beginning to come out. It needed some bastard like you to bring it out and I'm grateful to you for that.'

'We'll see, no, I will 'cos you won't be here.' There was a slight pause and when Red continued his voice was cold. 'I figure we've done enough talking so it's back to the house and wait.' Buck hesitated. 'Move!' rapped Red. His voice showed he would stand no nonsense and that it would be worse for Buck if he tried to resist. The ranch owner stepped forward slowly, watching Red for the slightest deviation of attention of which he might be able to take advantage. Red knew his thought and, when Buck reached him, he stopped him and held his gun hard against the rancher's side, while he reached with his free hand for the holstered gun and threw it across the stable. 'Right, the house.'

Red prodded him forward and Buck left the stable followed by the foreman whose gun never wavered in its aim at the middle of Buck's back.

As the two men left the stable Johnny crossed the loft to its doorway from where he could see them walk to the house. It would be easy to drop Red but with his Colt so close to Buck's back it was too risky, Red's finger might automatically pressure the trigger when he was hit. Johnny knew Buck would be safe until Red's sidekicks returned, it might be less risky to Buck if he made his play when the two men were back in the house.

Five minutes later Johnny was ready to make his move when the distant sound of horses held him back as he started to the ladder to the ground floor of the stable. Too late! The odds against him would soon be four to one.

He would have to reassess the situation and devise new tactics.

The pound of hooves grew louder. They were heading for the house. Suddenly the sound of a rifle shot startled Johnny. It was the last thing he expected to hear. It had come from the house which surprised him even more. The regular rhythm of the horses' approach was interrupted, it faltered, paused at stop and then broke out in a fast irregular beat bearing back and round to the rear of the stable.

Johnny was across the loft to the top of the ladder and, with Colt drawn, dropped on one knee to watch the doorway.

A few moments later, to Johnny's surprise Chris and Matt hurried into the stable. They half ran towards the doorway opposite the house.

'What's the move?' called Matt.

'Got to be careful not to endanger Pa,' replied Chris. The seriousness on his face betrayed the worry he was feeling over the position they were in.

'I'll take him.' The two men were startled by the unexpected voice coming from the loft. They swung round, their Colts ready to blast should this turn out to be a trick.

Johnny stood up and swung round on to the ladder. As he came down, the two surprised men came across the stable to join him.

'What're you doing here?' demanded Chris.

'And what about that branding? I figure you know I didn't do it.' Matt's voice was harsh with annoyance and Johnny figured he had to give an explanation to regain their trust.

'Red has a scheme to take over the Circle C and the Running W just as we figured might be the case, Matt. But Wade Gibson was prepared to take some action to try to flush Red into making a move and reveal his intentions. He asked me to help him. The branding was part of the scheme to discredit you, Matt, and then Kathy might be inclined to wed Chris or so we hope Red would think. Sorry we couldn't let you in on this but it would have meant play acting by some of you and Red might have seen through that.'

'I don't suppose Wade figured on my liking Rhona Webster.'

It was Johnny's turn to be surprised. 'No, he didn't.'

'Well, Red must have done 'cos he sent Slim, Chuck and Blackie to frame the homesteaders by planting meat from a Circle C steer on them so that they had an excuse for driving them off. So it happens I messed up that scheme and got Slim to talk. He told us about Red's ideas and that he was holding my Pa until Slim and the other two got back then he was going to be killed – an accident.'

'So Red was moving fast,' mused Johnny.

'Wade figured that, with Matt gone and a marriage between Kathy and Chris a possibility, Red would want Buck out of the way so he could start playing his hand once the marriage had taken place. So Wade sent me here to keep an eye on Buck and to see that no harm came to him.'

'You ain't done a good job,' spat Chris hotly. 'That rifle shot at us came from Red and he'll have my father in the house at his mercy.'

'Keep calm,' said Johnny trying to alleviate the young man's fears. 'I reckon your Pa will be safe enough. I overheard Red telling him that he was waiting for his sidekicks to return. Now he's seen you he'll figure things have gone wrong so he'll use your father as a hostage or more likely as barter in order to make his getaway.'

Chris frowned. 'Possible, I suppose.'

'More than likely,' agreed Matt.

'So what can we do?' queried Chris.

'One thing we don't do is give way to that bastard,' said Johnny. 'He won't stick by what he says. He doesn't know I'm here so, if you two can keep his attention, I figure I could get to the front of the house and take him.'

Chris, doubt in his mind, sought reassurance from Matt.

'I figure it's the only way. We have an advantage because he thinks there's only two of us.'

'All right,' agreed Chris, 'but be careful, my Pa ain't exactly in a cosy position.'

'Don't worry. You keep Red occupied.' Johnny gave Chris a friendly tap on the shoulder. He glanced at Matt. 'Sorry about the branding.'

'Couldn't figure it,' said Matt, 'especially as you were involved. Wade was taking a risk with Kathy's affections.'

'Sure, that's what I told him but he reckoned it was worth it to flush Red into the open.'

'It will have been if we get my Pa out of there safely,' cut in an anxious Chris.

'We will.' Johnny hurried to the back door

of the stable while Chris and Matt took up positions on either side of the doorway facing the house. They checked their Colts and loosed off two shots in the direction of the house. A rifle cracked angrily in reply.

The two men kept up the attention sapping fusillade of spasmodic shooting which enabled Johnny, after running directly away from the back of the stable, to circle, without being seen, to a position approaching the front of the house.

'He's a long time,' Chris called to Matt.

'He'll be using every precaution to maintain the element of surprise,' replied Matt and, seeing Chris' obvious impatience, added, 'Give him a chance, Chris. If anybody can pull this off Johnny can. Let's play our part.' Matt quickly loosed off another shot. Chris did likewise and they were both relieved when an answering shot came whining through the door. Red Segal's attention was still directed towards the stable.

Johnny approached the veranda at the front of the house cautiously. He drew his

Colt and stepped slowly on to the wood-work. A squeak now might prove fatal. Three careful steps took him to the front door. His hand closed round the knob and he turned it slowly. He pressured the door and was thankful to find it unlocked. He pushed it open gently and stepped into a hallway at the opposite side of which there was one door and Johnny guessed it led into the room from which Red was watching the stable. He started to step towards it but he froze when a voice called out.

'Chris! Chris! You hear me?'

'Sure I hear you. If you've harmed my father...' The interrupted voice was distant.

'Your Pa's all right, and will be if I get out of here. His life for my freedom. What do you say, Chris?'

There was no immediate reply. Johnny's brain raced. Surely Chris wouldn't be tempted to agree. He'd warned him about just such a situation. Chris must realise that Red wouldn't stick to that sort of arrangement. He'd want Buck along as a safety measure, to ensure he wasn't pursued and then, when he was certain he was clear, he'd kill Buck out of revenge.

'Don't trust him, Chris,' Matt urged.

'That's my Pa's life you're gambling with,' Chris retorted.

'Give Johnny a chance.'

'That's putting my father's life at greater risk.'

'Do you figure Red will keep his word?'

'I don't know.'

'Well I do. Your father's life won't be worth a cent once Red is safe.'

Chris looked puzzled. The dilemma was tearing at him. He had to make a choice. Was one way less risky than the other?

'If I agree you come out and leave my father in the house,' he shouted.

A harsh laugh answered him. 'Take me for a fool? I come out there alone and you'll gun me down. Your Pa rides with me, safety precaution. That way I'm sure you keep your part of the bargain.'

'And how will I know you'll keep yours?'

Chris called.

'You don't. You'll just have to trust me; after all I have the upper hand.'

Chris did not reply. His mind was awhirl as it fought for the right solution.

'Don't give way,' urged Matt.

Chris did not speak. He frowned and bit his lips anxiously. He knew he was gambling with his father's life. Why the hell had Wade Gibson got him into this position?

In the house Johnny was tense. He could sense Chris's dilemma and knew he had to act quickly. If Chris gave way to Red's demand then he may not have the chance to jump him for he felt certain that once the agreement had been arranged Red would keep Buck close to his Colt.

Johnny stepped for the door quickly. A floorboard squeaked and as Johnny flung the door open Red was already spinning round. His finger closed on the trigger but Johnny's bullet was already making its impact. Red staggered backwards. His rifle roared but his aim had gone and the bullet tore harmlessly into the wall. Red jerked under the tearing of a second bullet and was flung against the window. Glass shattered into hundreds of pieces as the bulky body pitched out.

The roar of guns jolted Chris out of his battle. 'Pa!' He feared the worst as he yelled and, without hesitation, hurled himself out of the stable and ran towards the house. Through his bemused mind he was aware of a body crashing through a window and he knew it was Red Segal but he still ran, anxious to verify that his father was safe. He burst into the house, with Matt not far behind, and pulled up sharply when he saw Johnny unfastening the rope which held his father to a chair.

'Pa, you all right?' Chris asked anxiously.

'Sure, but what I want is some explanation, how come this fella's coming in the front door to rescue me?'

'Red didn't know he was here keeping an eye on you, so we kept Red pinned down while Johnny got round to the front of the house.'

'Keeping an eye on me?' Buck demanded answers.

He got them quickly as the three men unfolded the story of the recent happenings, and a proud glance of approval was directed at Chris when Matt revealed how Chris had handled Red's sidekicks at the homesteaders' camp.

'Seems to me I've had my eyes closed,' said Buck when he heard everything. 'Good job Wade and Johnny were alert to what might happen. But I reckon he'll have to be bawled out for putting my life at risk.'

'And Kathy's affection,' put in Matt.

'Come on then, Matt, let's ride to see the old devil.' Buck started for the door but stopped and turned to face the others again. 'Got a better idea than bawling him out. We'll tell him the sooner a double wedding's fixed the better and...'

'And Johnny can be best man at both,' cut in Matt with a grin. 'All right Chris?'

'Of course,' agreed Chris. 'I've not seen much of Rhona but I have a feeling...' Chris smiled his thanks at his father.

'And I'll make Wade pay for playing around with Kathy's feelings and my life – I'm without a foreman so he can let me have Johnny. How about it?' He directed his question at Johnny.

'Nothing I'd like better,' smiled Johnny.

The publishers hope that this book has given you enjoyable reading. Large Print Books are especially designed to be as easy to see and hold as possible. If you wish a complete list of our books please ask at your local library or write directly to:

Dales Large Print Books
Magna House, Long Preston,
Skipton, North Yorkshire.
BD23 4ND

This Large Print Book, for people
who cannot read normal print,
is published under the auspices of
THE ULVERSCROFT FOUNDATION

... we hope you have enjoyed this book.
Please think for a moment about those
who have worse eyesight than you ...
and are unable to even read or enjoy
Large Print without great difficulty.

You can help them by sending a
donation, large or small, to:

**The Ulverscroft Foundation,
1, The Green, Bradgate Road,
Anstey, Leicestershire, LE7 7FU,
England.**
or request a copy of our brochure for
more details.

The Foundation will use all donations
to assist those people who are visually
impaired and need special attention
with medical research, diagnosis
and treatment.

Thank you very much for your help.